CYBORG DREAMS:
The Mind
Of Mine

To Ittay,

Keep programming!
I hope your bow+
arrow turns out
awesome!

H.A. Burns

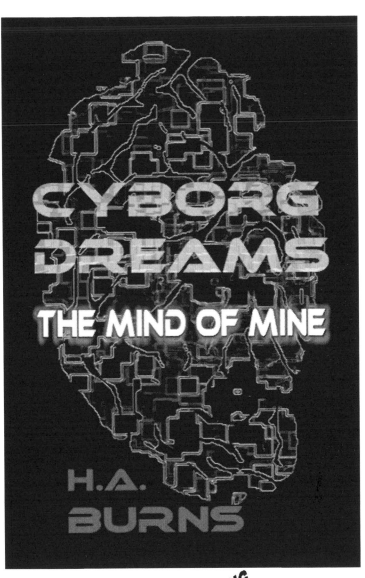

CYBORG DREAMS

THE MIND OF MINE

H.A. BURNS

ABSOLUTELY AMAZING eBOOKS

ABSOLUTELY AMAZING eBOOKS

Published by Whiz Bang LLC, 926 Truman Avenue, Key West, Florida 33040, USA.

For information contact:
Publisher@AbsolutelyAmazingEbooks.com

ISBN-13: 978-1945772740 (Absolutely Amazing Ebooks)

ISBN-10: 1945772743

I would like to dedicate this book to my friend Cliff Olmsted, who upon hearing about my crazy dreams told me I needed to write a book.

So, I did.

CYBORG DREAMS:
The Mind
Of Mine

PROLOGUE

Was this a dream? Really, it had to be! Catherine thought as she tried to blink away the lights flashing in a high school hallway full of books and people floating weightless and stunned. Her fellow teacher Elisabeth looked at her in horror and confusion, as if this was her fault! Just because the shadowy man at the end of the hallway was speaking to Catherine didn't mean she knew anything about anything.

The only thing Catherine knew was that even though this somehow wasn't a dream, the man at the end of the hallway was from a dream. A recurrent, bothersome dream that she had been having for months. Every time she awoke, all she could remember was that he had been standing there, staring at her and warning her of something. Now he was just yelling at her, that she hadn't listened and it was too late.

"Why can't this be a dream?" she thought.

Then it was over. The lights were back to normal, the man was gone, and everything (and everyone) fell to the floor with a thud and a few grunts. Elisabeth, the 10th grade geometry teacher who Catherine now knew had a mean scowl, was deadlocked looking at her for an explanation. Her gaze that could kill was interrupted by Jordan, a know-it-all history teacher who seized Catherine by the arm and dragged her to her feet. In an instant they were walking to the principal's office, as if she was in trouble.

"Jordan, did you see what I saw?" she asked.

A quick nod was all the reply she could get. Elisabeth was up and on her feet, marching right behind them, scowl gone and replaced with bewilderment.

"Do you think he will listen?" she said.

Catherine responded with, "I don't know why, he never listened to me before ..."

Jordon interrupted with, "Yes, but that was before the whole world was turned upside down in front of half the school. How can he not believe you? How can anyone?"

CHAPTER 1

Shake and Quake

Catherine Newton was a simple English teacher: mousy, skinny, dull-haired and neatly dressed. She led a simple life with her simple house on a hill overlooking the red rock valley of Desert Grande, Colorado.

Her greatest pleasure was driving the winding road down the hill into the valley to work every day. It was illegal to drive a vehicle in manual mode without an emergency, but the tracker software didn't work well on the hillside, so she got away with it if she remembered to shift to autopilot once she got to the main roads. That little bit of rebelliousness, coupled with the downhill speed, was better than coffee at waking her up and making her feel alive, and she truly needed something to make her feel alive.

It had only been six months since she got assigned to this little town in the middle of nowhere, and things were already starting to feel monotonous. Of course, every town was a little town in the middle of nowhere now. The war of 2020 decimated all the major cities in the US, so everyone was relegated to controlled population towns like Desert Grande, far from the obliterated coastlines and too small to be a target for any large missile strike. She certainly couldn't hope for a better town.

As Catherine drove onto the main road, hit the autopilot button and sat back in her car seat to stare out the window at the passing scenery, she couldn't help but feel out of place. The roads were so different here: all white and smooth. Such a huge contrast to the red rock and dirt of the surrounding desert.

The company, Greggo Sands, the heart of' this desert town, was responsible for the invention of the new ceramic roads. The roads harness energy from not only the seasons heating and cooling but the movement and weight of the cars on the road. It was enough to power the high school and other public buildings in the town. The company was proud of the model town and how successful the roads were implemented. Pretty soon the roads would be everywhere, so long as Greggo Sands could mine enough of the minerals they needed from the valley near Desert Grande.

Mining was constant, and small quakes from blasting could be felt in the school on a daily basis. Catherine was already used to the little quakes, and even slept right through a few major ones. She slept right through a lot of things lately, in fact her alarm this morning. She would be late for homeroom for the fourth time this month. Her sleep just wasn't what it used to be, waking dreams and nightmares of things she could not explain.

She arrived to the school, and had to slip in the back so that no one would see her coming in late. Thankfully, everyone was already in class. Her students were all busy on their assigned digital notebooks, the digiStudent Notebook, and they didn't even notice her enter the room. Catherine found her assigned digital notebook for teachers, the digiTeacher Controller, and did roll call. Only one student absent.

"Has anyone seen Jonny Ricker?" she asked.

Lucy Gamble, a little red-haired, freckled and constantly frazzled girl answered with "He's in the bathroom; I think he is sick." Jonny walked in before she could finish the sentence, waddling and holding his belly.

"Miss Newton, can I go to the nurse?" he asked.

"Of course, Jonny, let me mark your digiStudent so they know you were sent by a teacher."

As he leaned over to grab his notebook, the floor started to shake. Another quake, typical, or so they thought. But it kept going, and jerked both Catherine and Jonny to the ground as a loud ringing "BANG" reverberated throughout the walls and floor.

Jonny hit his head on the desk and was out cold. Catherine asked Lucy to help her get Jonny to his feet. He would need stitches now and was bleeding all over the place. Catherine set the main wall to show current events, News Channel 4, and announced, "I will quiz you on current events tomorrow, so pay attention."

If she left them with nothing, they would have gone wild for sure. It was all she could think of to do and maybe by the time she got back there would be an explanation of the explosion.

Dragging bleeding Jonny, with the help of wincing Lucy, down the hallway she ran into Jordan Muntz. Literally. He almost fell to the ground, but caught himself by clinging onto the lockers. He was a wiry middle-aged man who happened to be the most boring

History teacher in the world (according to a few of her students anyway).

"Watch it!" he yelled.

"Excuse me, but you ran into us," Catherine said as she wondered how in the world he could have missed seeing the three of them ambling through the hallway. She had been staring at the gaping wound in Jonny's head and didn't even see Jordan until he was bashed into the lockers.

Un-phased, he proceeded down the hall with what looked like purpose, though he always seemed to have purpose and authority like he owned the place.

Nurse Betty Green was old, kind, and going senile. She looked like something out of a cartoon, with pink hair and horned glasses. Her make-up was so caked it flaked and the red lipstick did nothing for her thin wrinkled lips but accentuate the depth of the wrinkles. Her smile was bright though, and so were her warm brown eyes as she peered over her digital reader to see the motley group enter her office.

Up on her little polka-dot-heeled feet like a rabbit, Betty jumped. She immediately went for the bandages in her drawer to stem the flow of blood coming out of Jonny's forehead. As Jonny sat on the medical bed, he asked in a concerned voice, "You aren't going to make me turn and cough, are you, Nurse Green?"

"Turn and cough? Why would I want you to cough, turn what? OH MY! No, we don't do those kinds of exams here, son. Why in the world would you think I would ask you to do that?!"

"Mr. Foster, my gym teacher did," Jonny alleged, looking down and away from Betty.

"He did what?!?" Betty exclaimed, stepping back at first then clasping little Jonny's hand to comfort him as she searched for what in the world to say next. Jonny giggled, unable to hold the ruse for too long. Then he winced, looked sickeningly green for a second, and then hurled right onto Betty's prize polka-dot shoes.

"He was feeling sick before he fell and hit his head in the quake. The bad jokes have nothing to do with any of it, although he has always had bad jokes," proclaimed Lucy. She looked like she was barely holding it together herself as she was compulsively poking at the blood on her shirt with a small cloth and trying not to look at the puke on the floor.

"Lucy, you can return to homeroom now," announced Catherine. "Thank you for helping out with Jonny today. I will give you a few merits on your digiStudent account when I get back."

Lucy looked relieved, then proud as she scurried away down the hall. Nurse Betty was busy vigorously cleaning up her antique, designer shoes. "No need to stay, Miss Newton," she stated. "He'll need stiches and he is running a pretty high fever. I've already sent the notification with details to the ambulance service."

"Betty, what about his parents? Should I notify them as well?" inquired Catherine.

"No, the system automatically notifies parents when an ambulance is called. Indeed, you can go unless you want to help me clean the nasty puke off of my shoes." With that, Catherine was out the door, opening it quickly just as Jordan walked by. The smack of him hitting the door was so hard it cracked the glass in the pane and left Jordan flat on his butt in the hallway right as the bell for class change rang. Students began milling out of the doors and rushing through the halls as he sat there stunned with Catherine looking over in shock, hands over her mouth, eyes wide.

"I'm so sorry, Jordan. I truly am not trying to beat you up today," declared Catherine, laughing incredulously.

"Why is that hard for me to believe?" he muttered as he pushed Catherine's helpful hands away. He managed to scramble up from the ground while being racked half a dozen times by careless student backpacks. "Good day," he said as he pushed his way through the crowded hallway.

Twice in one day! What are the odds? Catherine thought as she couldn't help but notice that Jordon looked atypically disturbed and disoriented. Being hit twice could do that, but maybe it was more than that. It might be the large quake. That was the biggest one Catherine had felt since coming to the desert. They were all from explosions at the mine, but this one felt different. As if something big was released and rumbled out after the initial bang. Maybe the news channel had covered it by now. She hurried down the hall to her classroom to see.

Her new class was settling into their seats, looking up at the north wall where the news was covering mosquitos at the lake, and the hazards of the Quinta virus. This new virus would start with a blackening welt at the site of a mosquito bite, and then move over the skin in small black lines that would leave a permanent scar if not treated immediately. It sounded horrifying but supposedly wasn't deadly, just ugly. Everyone was warned not to go near the lake until further fumigation efforts could completely eliminate the mosquito threat.

There was nothing on the news about the quake. Odd. She asked the new class if they had heard anything about the big bang. Rick Strand, a second-year senior and popular wisecrack, chimed in with, "Yeah, the big bang started the universe or something. Wait, aren't you an English teacher? Shouldn't we be learning how to read and write and stuff?"

As Catherine turned off the news and reached for her digiTeacher Controller, she wondered how in the world she ever ended up a high school English teacher. Dad. It was his fault. So easy to blame Dad. He always believed in her, told he she could be anything. Until he died when she was eleven, leaving her with nothing but a dog and a useless old diary. He had been a teacher too and, on some level, she was just trying to make him proud; to honor or memorialize him in some way. He lived through the great dust war, and managed to provide safety and security even after losing her mom in the initial LA blast. They had been on a fishing trip in Montana vising extended family when everything started. They were never even allowed back in LA to look for her mom. Catherine didn't remember any of it, she was only two at the time. She couldn't even remember her mom. But she remembered her father's pain and loneliness and would do anything to make him happy. Even become a teacher like him. How he did it she didn't know. She had only been a teacher for six months, and man, some of these kids were annoying!

Lunch couldn't come soon enough. Once the bell rang, she headed straight for the teacher's lounge. Elisabeth Gordan, the geometry teacher who she thought might be on drugs because she always seemed so happy, stepped up to her as soon as she walked in. Smirking, she said, "So I hear you knocked Jordan out, he looks pretty beat up. Good job!"

Elisabeth was obviously very entertained. She never liked Jordan; not many of the other teachers did either. He kept to himself and always seemed bored with everyone. Elisabeth was Catherine's only work friend. Actually, she was the only one who ever talked to Catherine. She was bright and bubbly, in her late 50s with graying black hair that had a white streak down the front. Blushing, Catherine said, "It was an accident, both times!"

"Both times?" Elisabeth laughed.

"Oh, so you are laughing about me now, great," interjected Jordan. He was tucked back in the corner next to the window with a bird's-eye view of the whole room. He did look pretty beat up; there was a purple welt on his head that was starting to look like an Easter egg. Catherine took some ice from the ice machine and a washcloth to bring to Jordan as a goodwill gesture. As she sat at his table and handed him the icy cloth, her mind suddenly went blank. Elisabeth sat down and looked at both Catherine and Jordan and laughed again, saying, "Twice? Please, do tell."

"Jordan was obviously distracted by something, Elisabeth. Else, he wouldn't have run into me and that door in one day if he were paying any attention at all. What I want to know, is what was so distracting?"

inquired Catherine. Jordon suddenly looked distraught.

"Was it the quake?" Catherine asked.

"What would make you think that?" Jordan replied.

"Just that it seemed bigger than normal. I know I have only been here a little while so I don't know much about the mining, but I don't think it should shake the entire school hard enough to knock people down."

"Who was knocked down?" Jordan responded.

"Me and my student Jonny, the one we were carrying to the nurse's office when you ran into us," Catherine answered.

"I didn't run into you, you ran into me," retorted Jordan.

"Yeah, and I ran the door into your head too. Come on! You were distracted. Why?" said Catherine.

"Look, he is obviously just clumsy and antisocial. Let's leave him alone," said Elisabeth.

"You didn't think the quake was weird, Elisabeth?" Catherine questioned.

"Yes, it did seem a bit stronger, but maybe they just had a big area they needed to collapse today," replied Elisabeth shrugging her shoulders. She smiled and waved at other teachers as they walked into the lounge, and seemed to be getting bored of the conversation. "Anyway, I can't believe the story about the Quinta virus. This is the fifth virus supposedly at the lake in the last few years. Who has ever heard of something that can leave black scars on your body? Now that is sick and twisted!"

9

"Don't believe everything you hear. Especially if it is about the lake. It has been closed off for over two years now with excuse after excuse and I don't buy any of it. It all seems fishy," said Jordan.

"The lake seems fishy?" Elisabeth couldn't help but smirk at her own joke. "Really, Jordan, the lake seems fishy?" She was trying not to laugh.

"Five viruses in just a few years? If it was a cover up, why wouldn't they just use the same virus? That is peculiar to say the least," pondered Catherine.

"The lake runs straight from the mine and they are just trying to cover up toxic spills," announced Jordan. "There are no viruses from mosquitos. It is a cover up."

"Again, if that was the case, why make up viruses?" replied Catherine.

"So, a conspiracy theorist, is that why no one likes you, Jordan?" asked Elisabeth rhetorically. "I think I have had enough of these fish tacos they keep serving us; hope they didn't get them from the lake," she stated as she got up and dumped the rest of her lunch in the trash. "Hope you don't get knocked out again, Jordan." She looked at Catherine and winked, "Remember, three strikes you're out," she said as she left the lounge with as smug a grin as anyone could manage.

"God, I hate her," Jordan said as she walked away.

"I sincerely am sorry about the lump on your head, Jordan. At least the ice seems to be getting the swelling down," insisted Catherine as she stabbed at her fish tacos with trepidation, wondering if, in fact, the fish had come from the lake. *Would the Quinta virus infect fish too?* she thought. She then held a piece of fish in the air, looking for black streaks.

"Don't worry, the fish come from a farm down in Clarksdale," said Jordan. "Elisabeth knows that and she was just messing with you."

"Are you sure? She is quite the character. Sometimes I wonder if she is on drugs. She sure is in a good mood all the time," replied Catherine. "That can't be normal for a teacher."

"And I am in a bad mood all the time. Do you think I am on drugs too?" said Jordan.

"Yes, of course" she replied quickly and sarcastically. Jordan smiled for the first time, maybe ever, as far as Catherine knew. Despite the lump on his head, he actually seemed handsome. It didn't last long though; he went right back to his vacant brooding.

"Where were you headed when you ran into us the first time today?" asked Catherine.

"You mean when you knocked me into the lockers? I was headed to the principal's office. I just had to ask him a question," stated Jordan. "Thank you for the ice, not so much for the lump." Another brief smile, and with that he was off in his usual hurry.

Maybe it was that smile, but it made her look at him differently. He was probably almost twice her age, early forties? Dark hair, olive skin, an unmistakable Italian nose, and matching attitude. She had never met a patient Italian. It is a wonder he had the fortitude for teaching, much less to high schoolers. He didn't seem like he belonged here. Catherine didn't feel like she belonged here either. *What a pair they would be*, she thought. That was a disturbing thought! Wow, she had a boyfriend! One that was her age and didn't make everyone want to sit on the other side of the room.

Her boyfriend, Anthony Grant, was sweet, kind, handsome, and hard working. They met at an outdoor concert in the park a few months ago when his dog tried to eat the entire contents of her picnic basket. She always liked fluffy puppies and fell in love with the dog immediately: they had the same taste in food, after all. It was Anthony that she wasn't sure about yet.

Anthony's family was assigned to Desert Grande a few years ago from an Ohio city that had become too overcrowded due to the bustling population of Catholics in the area. Three sisters, two parents, an Aunt, and two cousins all came here at once. She envied his big family, and loved his parents who took her in as one of their own. Catherine was starting to realize she liked his family and his dog more than him though, and didn't know how to handle the situation. She was having dinner with him tomorrow night, alone. No dog, no family. She could focus on him and maybe develop her feelings more.

The final bell for the day tolled its blessed release. Catherine got into her car, set the destination to home and set the car to autopilot. One of her favorite activities during the drive home was picking dinner for the night. The sooner she made the selection, the sooner the combinator would have it ready for her when she got to her house. Chicken enchiladas? Lasagna? Tuna casserole? Her go-to favorite was spaghetti and meatballs, which was also her dog's favorite.

Her fluffy white poodle Sass would be waiting for her, and probably was still shaking from the huge quake today. She deserved a treat. *Spaghetti and meatballs, it is!* Catherine thought as she entered the order selection. That would make Sass's day.

As she walked in the door she was greeted with a facial from Sass and the yummy smell of spaghetti in the kitchen. There was a vase shattered on the floor and in the hall way there was a large yellow puddle (courtesy of the poodle) that were likely the result of the scary big bang from the mine. She ordered the Roomba to fix the mess and went straight for the kitchen to pour herself a glass of red wine.

She remembered a time when there were things like refrigerators, ovens or a microwave in a kitchen. Now they were all one item, called a combinator. Basically, you inserted ingredients into the side, entered the bar code for the item and the combinator could offer a selection of meals based on overall contents. It knew cooking times and temperature, self-cleaned and even threw out expired items automatically. All you had to do was grab a utensil and open the door in the front when you were ready to eat your order. Whoever came up with this was living the life somewhere, probably in Oklahoma where all the cleanest land was after the war. It was one of the few places the fall-out dust never reached.

She sat down in her big, downy and comfy couch and offered a few meatballs to the dog. She then leaned back and put her feet up on the coffee table, sighing in comfort as she sipped her wine. She realized her car was automated, her food was automated, and her cleaning was automated. But, one thing that she wished she could automate was checking her student's writing assignments. Sure, spelling and grammar would auto-correct, but not content or proper use of a word. Forty students each class, 6 classes, and with two assignments a week meant her day was just starting when she got home. Spaghetti, and a large glass of red wine would get her through the evening. She snatched up her digiTeacher Controller and began to grade.

Sleep came pretty readily to Catherine. Especially after the tenth paper on how football was the greatest sport ever invented. Rarely did she even make it up to bed before she fell asleep during the school week, and tonight was no exception.

She always had such vivid dreams. Tonight, she was flying. She felt the warm wind in her hair and on her skin. She tasted the dewy tendrils of fog on her lips. The sky was a million colors coalescing into a morning sunrise of oranges faded to dark blue. She smiled as she saw a white-tailed bunny jump in the meadow as her feet landed on the soft, green grass. She turned to her left as she heard the movement of water, with little splashes as it hit the small wooden boat. The splashes and waves were sending up sparkles in the moonlight. She was at the lake in Desert Grande. Suddenly she was worried about the Quinta virus. *Did mosquitos like to bite early in the morning?* she thought. *Wait, this was a dream, mosquitos don't bite in dreams if you're in control!* She knew she was always in control. She walked over to the pier and sat down to watch the water caress the dock as the fog crawled over the lake breaking into little branches, like fingers.

"I thought I would find you here," said a voice that was all too familiar.

Catherine turned to see the man who had been haunting her dreams lately. She had never met him in real life that she could remember and had no idea who he was. His eyes were so different. Where there should have been pupils there was what looked like golden lenses that flashed strange symbols in the low light. Half of the top of his head was shaved and the other half was capped with what looked like a metal plate. He had rusty brown hair in his goatee and for his eyebrows. He wore a black turtleneck, slacks and gloves so that his entire body was covered from the neck down.

He walked straight up to her with almost a rhythmic pulse, as if his legs were mechanical. He put one hand on her arm and said the all too familiar words, "You have to stop the mining."

"Why? Who are you? How?" asked Catherine, as usual.

"You know I can't tell you. You know you can stop it, Catherine," he said, emphatically.

"Why can't you tell me? I don't even think you are real," she retorted.

"I am real, and I want to sleep. Today was close, they have found another lab. This is getting very dangerous for everyone. You do not want to wake me. You irrefutably don't want to wake my brother."

"Your brother?" she queried, standing up and walking towards him. She wanted to reach out and touch him, to see if he was really there.

"I have said too much. Just stop the mining. I have to go," he announced.

15

There was a bright flash, so bright it hurt her eyes. As she turned away she was jolted awake. Why did she have such weird dreams? Why couldn't she just dream of nice meadows and hopping bunnies and not mechanically enhanced guys trying to tell her what to do? It was 2 a.m. If she went back to sleep now she could get a few more hours before the daily grind. As she climbed the stairs to go to her bed, dog at her feet, she asked, "You don't dream about cyborgs, do you, Sass?" The confused little "woof" reply confirmed it: she was going crazy.

CHAPTER 2

Date of Mine

Anthony was late. He was never late. Maybe he was breaking up with her? Catherine thought as she was sitting at the restaurant, staring at her phone band on her left arm, trying to figure out what went wrong. The earlier text to confirm the time/location for their date was pretty straightforward, at least that is what she thought. Her text "Maggiano's, 6?" and his reply "Yes, Babe, CU tonight" couldn't be clearer.

It was 7 p.m. and she had already gone through two glasses of wine and what seemed like a loaf of bread that the waitress just kept filling back up in the center of the table. The tall, young, blonde waitress was well past annoyed and barely hiding it behind a thin smile which made Catherine cringe every time she came by to fill the bread and ask if she wanted more wine.

She had never been stood up before in her life! Should she leave? Wait an hour? Camp out? She had already texted him she was here; she didn't want to be nagging, especially if this was his way of breaking up. She didn't want him to know he upset her; she wanted to be tough!

Anthony walked through the door right as Catherine was getting up and had given up. He waived to her across the restaurant and she sat down with a huge sigh of relief. She didn't know who looked more delighted, her or the waitress. Anthony looked like he had just gotten out of the shower. His hair was slicked back and his skin still looked a little wet. He was dressed nice though, wearing a pressed, white-collared shirt and some pleated grey slacks. He always wore a gold cross on a chain at his neck, a sign of his Catholic heritage which he was more than serious about. Once he had told her the only reason he didn't become a priest was because he wanted a family of his own. He was 6'2", broad shouldered and knew how to turn heads in a room with a smile.

"I am so sorry, Babe," he said with a kiss on her cheek as he sat down across the table from Catherine. "Work kept me late and I was so upset and was rushing to get out of there to get to you that I left my phone band in my locker. I hurried as fast as I could," he said sincerely and then directed to the waitress, "Maim, we'll have an order of calamari for the table and another glass of wine for my beautiful, extra patient girlfriend."

"Coming right up," she replied as she put a thumbs-up behind Anthony, mouthing "Nice catch!"

Catherine couldn't help but blush. She wasn't used to dating handsome men. She wasn't used to dating in general. She had always been a bit of a reclusive bookworm. To have a guy like Anthony notice her was an adventure to say the least, and she was always getting comments from other women about his looks that made her feel a bit uncomfortable.

"I've already had two glasses of wine, Anthony. You know I am a lightweight," Catherine said.

"Oh, you are? Then this will be a cheap date," Anthony said with a smile that lit up his warm brown eyes and made Catherine wonder how she could be mad at him for anything, ever. But, he had stood her up for what felt like all night, so she couldn't just let him slide.

"Cheap date? No, I don't think so, Mr.! I plan to order heavy and make you pay. I will take it back home in a doggy bag for Sass. Those extra hours you worked today should cover it, right?" she asked, playfully.

Anthony laughed, "Well, I knew I would have to pay somehow. I am probably getting off too easy."

"Yes, way too easy, you big meany!" exclaimed Catherine.

"Believe me, I would have rather been here with you than at the mine this afternoon. There was a corridor that collapsed and trapped four guys inside. It took us two hours to clear it and by then, one of the crew was dead from bleeding out. I had to carry him out to medical myself. I've never seen anything like it, and I've worked with all of those guys for years. I actually did a work study stint with the guy who died, Larry Armstrong. He had three kids and even goes to my church."

"Wow, Anthony, I am so sorry to hear that. Has anything like this ever happened before at the mine?" she wondered.

"No, not that I know of, but these corridors where we are mining are very unstable. There are older structures that we keep running into lately. It seems the ancient people who lived here, supposedly a very long time ago, had created tunnels throughout this area right through the bedrock the company is interested in digging up. Ancient Navajo, supposedly. Yesterday I swear it looked like a laboratory though. I mentioned that it didn't look like Native American digs to me but my supervisor said these were Navajo tunnels and that it was impossible that they had labs."

"A lab? What makes you think it was a lab?" she asked, intrigued.

"Well, mind you I didn't get there until an hour after the blast, but there seemed to be broken glass on the ground and what looked like areas cut out of the rock for large rectangular objects. You know, like in the shape of those old refrigerators that they used to use to cool stuff," Anthony replied.

"Were there any electrical outlets or ventilation hoods built into the walls? Navajo's definitely didn't have those," she inquired.

"I don't remember seeing anything like that, no. I didn't think of that. You are so smart," he stated with a smile and clutched her hand from across the table. He had such big, strong hands.

Right then the calamari showed up and the waitress almost put the plate right where their hands had been, they had to quickly release before the plate came down. "What can I get for you two lovebirds?" she asked while looking at Anthony coyly. She was blatantly flirting!

"I'll have the surf and turf and this lovely young lady will have the chicken alfredo, extra parmesan," proclaimed Anthony with confidence as he handed the waitress the menus, not even giving her a glance. The waitress stomped away, a little peeved to be ignored.

"You know my order, do you?" asked Catherine playfully. Deep down she was a little put off though;

that wasn't what she wanted. She actually wanted the beef and spinach ravioli tonight but didn't want to embarrass Anthony, and she especially didn't want to call the waitress back.

"Of course I know your order. You always get the cheesiest item on the menu," he responded, jokingly.

She smiled and then looked down at her napkin that she had begun to toy with. It was little things like the wrong order that made her question her relationship. He acted like he knew her so well, but she felt like he didn't know her at all.

"Want to go on an adventure?" he asked, out of the blue.

She must have been showing some brooding on her face, because he obviously wanted to cheer her up. "What kind of adventure?" she said, taking the bait.

"Well, breaking and entering, with intent to take something," he said with a twinkle in his eyes, leaning forward with excitement.

"I would rather not go to jail, thank you very much. What would my students think?" she replied. She knew he would never steal; what was he up to?

"That you are a badass teacher," he said.

"Oh yeah, me a badass!" she retorted.

"Seriously though, I need to get my phone band. They are closing the mine for a few days until after Larry's funeral and I don't think I can survive without it. Want to go with me to the mine to get it?" he asked.

"You are serious?" she replied, curious.

"Yeah, it is not really breaking in though. I have an ID pass. I just said that to get your adrenaline pumping and bring out those rosy cheeks," he said as he slid his finger across her cheek and down her neck, making her blush. "It is not actually stealing either because it is my phone, but it would be an adventure."

"Ok, I am in as long as I don't have to wear a hardhat or anything," she responded.

"You would look extra cute in a hardhat; are you sure?" he asked, lightheartedly.

"Yes, it would mess up my hair," she said while putting her hands through her long brown hair and then flipping it to one side with a sigh.

They laughed and enjoyed the meal, gathering up two large doggie bags for the road when it was done. Anthony left a nice tip for the waitress, who Catherine caught checking out his butt on the way out. He never encouraged her though, which was one thing she liked about him. He was very loyal and never once made her question if he would cheat on her.

As they got to Anthony's car, he grabbed her by the waist and brought her close to him. He was so big and strong and her heart couldn't help but skip a beat or two as he kissed her passionately. Maybe it was the three glasses of wine, but she felt a bit dizzy and almost fell over when he let her go. He quickly gripped her and asked if she was all right.

"You took my breath away," she said wistfully. So, he kissed her again until her knees buckled and he slid her into the car with a laugh.

Catherine had never been to the mine before. She knew it was upstream from the lake, north of the main town and near the east red rock mountains. It was past 9 p.m., and dark, so she didn't see much on the trip up. Not that she would have been able to anyway; Anthony loved to make out in the car with it set to autopilot. By the time they reached the mine the windows were all fogged up and Anthony had to put the wipers on and roll the windows down in order to see to park.

"Let's go to the back entrance. It is closer to the lockers," he whispered as he held her hand and led her towards a path that went up to a cliff face.

"Are you sure this is okay, Anthony?" Catherine asked, looking around at the empty, dimly lit parking lot.

"Yes, don't worry so much. It's an adventure, remember?" he replied.

They went around to a dusky red door with bright yellow reflective tape along the edges that looked like it was built directly into the rocks. Once inside, Anthony turned on a flashlight and seized Catherine by the hand to lead her down an extended, shadowy corridor.

The air was cool but stale and smelt like dust and copper pennies. *It was so quiet!* Catherine thought. The only sound was the shuffle of their feet and what seemed like humming from something far down the passage. When they reached the end, it opened up into a large room with lockers all around and a circular washing station in the center. The humming she had heard earlier was coming from a dim yellow light hanging in the center of the room. There were three more corridors to the right, one had yellow caution tape in the shape of an X covering the entrance.

"Is that the corridor that collapsed today?" asked Catherine.

"You would think that, but no. That caution tape is covering the entrance to the corridor leading to the area I thought was a lab. They closed it off at the end of the day yesterday," stated Anthony. "The area that collapsed today is closed off too, but further down. It is down the first corridor to the right."

Anthony opened his locker and pulled out his phone band, gave it a little kiss and put it back on his left arm. He looked so handsome in the dim light, and the adrenaline from sneaking into the mine was going to Catherine's head.

"You know, wouldn't it be sexy to do it right here, right now?" Catherine whispered as she pushed him against the locker and rubbed her hands down his muscled chest.

"Yes," he said catching his breath between kisses. As her hand caressed his stomach and then began to descend, he grabbed her hand. "But, I am saving myself until marriage; you know how important my faith is to me, Catherine. Please respect that," he pleaded.

"I wasn't serious. I'm sorry if you thought I was," she said and stopped what she was doing immediately. Catherine felt what she always felt when he said those words: frustrated and ashamed. She did not share his faith, but respected his strength in his beliefs. She wasn't a virgin either, and was not used to the reverse situation where the guy was not pressuring her. The way he made out with her all the time left her very flustered to say the least. It was easy for her to forget about his faith in the moment, but he held strong despite her advances. It blew her mind that he was 22 and a virgin still. She had to think of something to change the subject.

"Can we go to your 'lab'? Maybe check for electrical outlets and ventilation shafts?" she inquired.

"Sure, I don't mind breaking some rules every now and then, Babe. Plus, wouldn't it be crazy if there was an electrical outlet in a supposed, 'Navajo tunnel'?"

Catherine wanted to know too. Anthony saying that he found a lab yesterday reminded her of her dream last night. She was curious if it was a lab, maybe her dream was true? The bizarre man in her dream did mention a lab. Up until now, she just thought that the whole time she was dreaming about this cyborg guy telling her to "stop the mining" it had to do with her subconscious not liking all the quakes. That made complete sense to her, and she had a vivid imagination, so he could easily fit into her dark dream world.

"Let's be bad asses, Babe," Anthony decreed as he removed the caution tape and clutched Catherine by the hand. He led her down a dark passage for what felt like a half hour.

"You see this stuff in the side of the rock here," he said as he flashed the light to what looked like grey stone with embedded copper pennies, except they weren't pennies they were just odd shaped circles in the rock that were darker than the adjacent rock. "This is bauxite; it is what we are mostly mining for the ceramic roads we're building. They use that and the gadolinite found in the other mine, of course, to get all the elements they need."

Catherine was not a scientist, and knew nothing about rocks or mining. Science was too cut and dry, no room for creative interpretation or fun. Where was the fantasy in rocks? She could imagine rock giants exchanging money in rock pennies in the wall, and that was far more fun. A good fiction book, to escape her boring life, that is what she was interested in the most. But, she nodded and said, "Pretty neat stuff" because Anthony was obviously fascinated by the rocky walls that his hands were caressing as if they were her body. Further down they finally came to another opening.

"This is it," was all Anthony said as he moved the flashlight around the room. There was still broken glass on the ground.

"Stop. Let me see that," Catherine asserted as she reached for the flashlight. On the ground were lines, exactly two feet apart coming from one of the rectangular holes and leading back down the way they came as if something had been dragged away. Further inspection found a small circular hole in the back of the rectangular cut out.

"There was obviously something here that was drug out and why would the Navajo create a perfectly rectangular indent in the rock with a small hole in the back?" asked Catherine.

"Yeah, something about the cuts in the wall, they look machined. That small hole could be an outlet but, unfortunately, I don't see any electrical wiring. Didn't you say something about a lab needing a ventilation shaft? I don't see one of those either," proclaimed Anthony as he pointed the flashlight to the ceiling and moved it along slowly as if looking for something.

"The ventilation shaft could be anywhere. It doesn't have to be above us. They could have used a fan and moved the air downward, or even sideways. Plus, couldn't it be closed off, full of rubble from the blast?" asked Catherine.

"See, this is why I love you. You're so smart!" Anthony exclaimed with a kiss and a hug that lifted Catherine off of her feet.

Catherine was in shock. He had never said he loved her; this was the first "I love you" between them and she didn't know what to say. She knew one thing: she did not love him, at least not yet. *Maybe it was a figure of speech and not a real "I love you." Maybe she should just ignore it?*

"So, what do you think they drug out of here? A refrigerator?" she asked, quickly trying to distract Anthony.

"I don't know, but whatever it is, it had to be pretty heavy to leave those marks in the rock." He took the flashlight from Catherine and declared, "Look, over here, another one," as he walked across the room towards another rectangular hole in the wall.

"Where does that tunnel go?" she enquired as she moved his hand to point down a long, roughly hewn tunnel to the left.

"I don't know. Honestly, there is a lot I don't know around here. I'm nothing more than a simple miner, after all. We should probably head out. I can ask when I get back to work about the lines on the ground and the small holes in the walls. Maybe someone will know. It doesn't look like Navajo work to me, but what do I know, right?" he pondered out loud.

"Okay, lead the way, Babe," Catherine said as she took his arm. She was seriously regretting wearing heels to her dinner date at this point. They weren't quite right for the spelunking adventure it had turned into and her feet were killing her.

"So, what if it is a lab, what do you think that means, Anthony?" she queried as they were winding their way through the passageways in the dark.

"I don't know. Honestly, I never thought that far ahead," he replied. He seemed distracted by something.

"What's the matter, Anthony?" she asked.

"I'm sorry, but, I have to say it. I do love you, Catherine. I love how smart you are and how you analyze everything. I love your dimples and doe eyes, and the way you flip your hair when you're nervous. Don't you love me too?" he pleaded as he flashed the flashlight right in her face. She couldn't help but laugh. Then he did too. The sudden spotlight just highlighted how pointed and substantial the question he asked was, and how awkward of a situation to be in when he asked her.

"What I would love is to be out of these heels and back in the car making out some more," she exclaimed as she gave him a kiss on the cheek and moved the flashlight to show her heels on the rocky floor.

They walked in silence though the tunnels in the dark and finally out of the door in the mountainside. When they got in the car, Anthony set the automatic pilot to go back to the restaurant where Catherine's car was waiting. As he rubbed her feet on the drive, he looked up at her with puppy dog eyes and asked, "Will you answer my question now?"

"How could I not love you, you're amazing. Tall, sexy, hardworking and the sweetest man I have ever met," she replied with as big a smile as she could muster. All of it was true, so she wasn't lying. She felt bad though, because she had made it sound like she was saying she loved him without actually saying she loved him. Truthfully, she asked herself the same thing: how could she not love him? But she didn't love him, and it was confusing.

"I am so glad you said that, because there is something else I wanted to ask you, Catherine," he proclaimed.

Right then her heart stopped. *This could not be happening. I mean, she kind of expected it given his faith and the fact that he introduced her to his whole family on the third date. But, it had only been four months! Now?!? She wasn't ready for a proposal!*

"Can you watch Rufus for me this weekend? I have a hunting trip with some of the guys from work and I don't trust my sisters with my dog. Last time Gretchen and Ariana watched him we found him two days later in a landfill eating out of old diapers."

Suddenly Catherine questioned how much she liked Rufus. *Eating WHAT out of a landfill? How many times had he licked her face?*

"Of course, Babe, anything," she replied. "Sass will be happy to have the company."

They arrived at Maggiano's at around 11 p.m. It was another 20 minutes until Catherine would be home. It was another 30 minutes before she was in bed after taking a thorough shower to get rid of all the tunnel dust on her clothes. She couldn't help but focus on the time, she had to be up at 6 to get ready for school. But, she just couldn't sleep. She lay there in bed, staring at the alarm clock wondering how she got to where she was: lying to a man that loved her, unable to love him back.

What was wrong with her? So, he ordered her chicken alfredo instead of ravioli; the chicken alfredo was delicious. Did that mean he didn't know her? No. But, he also didn't ask about her day, in fact he rarely asks her anything about herself. She knew everything about him, and loved all that she knew. He just liked to talk a lot, and joke a lot, which dominated the conversation. He was so charming. Did she need anything more?

Maybe she just needed to talk more? Maybe tell him about herself instead of waiting for him to ask? At least he didn't ask her to marry him tonight! What would she have said? If she had said yes, she would be lying. If she had said no, would he have broken up with her? She didn't want to break up. She loved his parents and his dog Rufus and would miss them dearly.

This whole Catholic thing bothered her a little bit too. *Would she have to convert to Catholicism?* They hadn't even talked about that yet. He probably expected kids right away, and she knew Catholics were against birth control so that meant they would have as many kids as he wanted. She loved kids, and he was handsome, so they would have beautiful children. *But, how many did she want?*

After the war, the vast majority of the population was gone and what was left was encouraged to rebuild. The government had incentives if you wanted kids. She could quit her boring job and just make babies for a living if she married Anthony. The government would pay her to have kids and stay home with them, and Anthony's parents were constantly talking about grand kids. *Would her dad be proud of her if she quit being a teacher?*

The alarm clock was buzzing. It was 6 a.m. already. She hadn't slept a wink. It was going to be a rough day at work!

CHAPTER 3

Merits of Merits

Homeroom went by in a blur. At the bell Lucy asked about her merits for helping with Jonny the other day. Catherine had forgotten to post them to her account with all the commotion of hitting Jordan with the nurse room door and then the news of the Quinta virus at the lake. She gave Lucy 1 extra merit for reminding her and 2 merits for the help with Jonny. When the merits registered into Lucy's digiStudent account, Catherine also had to congratulate Lucy on her silver level merit achievement. Lucy must be quite the teacher's pet to get to that level, maybe that was why she was always in a frazzle.

"Class, please give Lucy a round of applause; she is now a silver level student!" Catherine announced to the room Lucy blushed as the students gave her a standing ovation. Most of the class was up anyway to leave because the bell had already rung but the sincere ovation still surprised Catherine. This was the first any student she had even came close to silver, so she had no idea how the other students would react to the required announcement. It was amazing how supportive everyone was for Lucy.

"Keep up the good work. You still have time to reach gold before the end of the semester," said Catherine. Lucy gave Catherine a look of determination in a quick smile as she hurried off to her next class.

It took 500 points in one semester to get to silver level; gold was 700. Most students earned less than 200. Academics were rewarded of course, with an A standing for the semester generating 50 points per class, a B 30, C 20, D 10 and F -10. So even with trending straight A's, 100 points are still needed to get to silver. These additional points are achieved through joining extracurricular sports or clubs, volunteer efforts and philanthropy. Each sport is 10 points, so is each club. Presidents and heads of teams and clubs got an additional 5 points. Student body government is 20 for president, and 15 for vice president, and 10 for each member of the board. Helping teachers, running food drives for those less fortunate, bake sales to raise money for band equipment, etc. ... counted as philanthropic endeavors and could generate up to 10 points each semester.

Not only did silver and gold level standing look good on a college resume, but it afforded perks at the school as well. Silver level were able to walk the halls without a teacher endorsement on their digiStudent account and could miss a class for a week without penalty so they could study in the library or work on other philanthropic endeavors. There was also a preferred line at the cafeteria for all silver and gold level students, with extra dessert options.

Catherine knew how the system worked, but couldn't seem to get more students active in earning merits. No one seemed to want to put in efforts past the minimum. The teacher whose homeroom students had the most merits was given a small bonus with a little money to throw a congratulatory party for the students at the end of the semester. Catherine was always a bit competitive and always wanted to win. However, even with Lucy's silver level merit status, her classroom was nowhere near the top performers in the school. Elisabeth probably knew how to motivate students.

When lunch came, Catherine headed straight to the teacher's lounge. Japanese Udon noodles was the special of the day, and the line was long at the faculty combinators. She spent the time in line analyzing the merits of her homeroom class, picking out top performers to hone.

"How do I get my students to want to achieve more merits?" she immediately asked Elisabeth as soon as she was finally able to sit at her table.

Elisabeth had been reading a book while nibbling on what looked like a whole wheat cucumber sandwich that she must have brought from home. From her posture, Elisabeth was deliberately ignoring the two other teachers at the table. The two other teachers looked like they were in a heated discussion, but one of them glanced at Catherine when she sat down and scoffed at Catherine's question before returning to her conversation. Elisabeth laughed at the scoff.

"High school is hard enough without the pressure of merits, Catherine. Why would you want your students to achieve more?" she retorted.

"I like the idea of throwing them a little party, plus I like to win," Catherine responded earnestly.

"Aren't you sweet," replied Elisabeth. "I wouldn't worry about it though. The same teacher has been winning every semester since it started 4 years ago, and I don't think she will be bested by a newbie."

"Who wins it?" Catherine asked. She heard scoffing again from the debating duo sitting with them at the table, as if the question was dumb.

"You're looking at her kid," said Elisabeth, with a mischievous grin.

Catherine was beat red with embarrassment. She should have known Elisabeth would be the top teacher in the school. "So, I don't suppose you would want to divulge any secrets as to how you managed to get the students more involved?" Catherine pleaded.

"Honestly? No. Not that I think you are much competition, but I like to win too, and giving away secrets is not how you win" she replied as she finished off her cucumber sandwich in one large bite.

"I see. Well, I might be competition. I had one student reach silver level today," Catherine countered, hoping to get a response out of Elisabeth.

"Who?" Elisabeth queried, suddenly no longer gloating.

"Lucy Gamble," Catherine proclaimed proudly, then added, "The whole class gave her a standing ovation when they heard. I was surprised."

"I see. Why were you surprised? That is quite an achievement."

"I was surprised because when I went to school, the kids who did well were picked on, not applauded," Catherine replied.

"Did you think that maybe one of the reasons everyone is encouraging to Lucy is because her father is a foreman at the mine? He could fire half their dads and they would be on the street or reassigned to another city. You didn't know that, did you? The ties to the mine control a lot of things around here, Catherine."

"I guess there are a lot of things I don't know. Josh Armstrong was out of class today. I just realized Larry Armstrong must be his father, right?" Catherine asked.

"Yes, why do you ask?"

"My boyfriend said Larry died yesterday at the mine in a collapsed corridor. They are closing the mine until Monday for his funeral on Sunday. You didn't see it on the news last night?" Catherine inquired.

"Yes, I did. But, I didn't realize the man that died had a son in high school. That is very sad. Do you plan on going to the funeral? Did you need someone to go with you?" asked Elisabeth.

"I hadn't thought of that. I will be watching my boyfriend's dog Rufus this weekend and I don't want to leave him at the house alone with my dog Sass," Catherine responded.

"I forgot you had a boyfriend. How is that handsome young Anthony? If only I were 30 years younger, you would have some competition there too," Elisabeth proclaimed with a smile and a wink.

"He is fine, handsome as ever. He was part of the crew that pulled Larry from the rubble. He isn't even going to the funeral. I guess his hunting trip that he's been planning with his buddies is more important."

"Hunting trip?" inquired Jordan as he sat down next to Catherine. The dynamic duo of arguing teachers had just gotten up and left, leaving room. Jordan seemed less forlorn and gloomy than usual as he pushed aside the dirty napkin left on the table to make room for his cup of Udon noodles. She had never seen him purposely sit next to anyone before, this was new.

"Catherine was just telling me about her boyfriend Anthony, and how is he going on a hunting trip this weekend and leaving her with his dog Rufus," said Elisabeth. "Your head is looking better Jordan, though that isn't saying much."

"Thank you for your kind words, as usual, Elisabeth," Jordan rejoined, casually ignoring the insult. "It takes a year to get a license to hunt anything other than fish around here, and then there are limited windows for hunting specific game. Elk, for instance, is only in October for two weeks. That is probably what he will be hunting this weekend."

"If I wanted a boring lecture, Jordan, I would take your class," Elisabeth said as she got up to leave. "Tell Lucy congratulations on the silver merit achievement for me, Catherine. You'll need four more in your class if you plan to come anywhere near close to me in winning the homeroom party merit reward," she declared as she patted Catherine on the back and left with her typical grin.

"Four more silver level students? How in the world does she do it?" Catherine pondered aloud, incredulous.

"She is lying, as usual, she likes to pull your leg if you haven't noticed," said Jordan.

"Really? Why do I always fall for it then?" replied Catherine.

"Because you are young and naïve," stated Jordan, casually.

"Thanks," Catherine answered as she was starting to understand why Jordan sat alone most days. "Thanks for the explanation about the hunting as well. I was starting to think Anthony was a bit callous for not going to his co-worker's funeral."

"So, your boyfriend works at the mine in the tunnels then?" asked Jordan.

"Yeah, he loves rocks. I mean, really loves rocks! I didn't realize how much until I saw him caressing a tunnel wall last night," she replied.

"You went to the mine last night?" exclaimed Jordan, looking shocked and somewhat angry. "Do you realize how dangerous that was? The tunnels are very unstable. The blasting they are doing is not safe. Did that not register in your pretty little head when you heard a man died there yesterday?"

Catherine felt reproached, and a bit indignant. It truly did not occur to her the mines could be unstable when no one was there and there was no mining going on.

"We were the only ones there. It seemed all right to me," she declared.

"What were you doing there?" Jordan questioned.

"I wanted to see something," Catherine responded.

"What?" Jordan asked. "Please, tell me what could have possibly persuaded you to enter a dangerous mine in the middle of the night."

Catherine wasn't sure how to answer the question. *Should she tell him about her dreams and that strange mechanically enhanced man and his inane warnings to stop the mining? How he had said they had found another lab and she wanted to see if there was a lab in the mine just so she could prove whether or not the man in her dreams was real?* She didn't know what sounded more insane: dreaming of cyborgs or thinking a man from her dreams might be real. As she opened her mouth to try and explain, the bell rang for class.

"Another time then," Jordan stated as he quickly devoured his bowl of noodles, then jumped up to leave. "You look awful today, by the way. You should try getting some sleep instead of running around in mining tunnels trying to get yourself killed. What do they call it? Beauty sleep? It would help with the dark circles under your eyes," and with those words of wisdom he was gone.

Catherine got up to go to her next class. It would be medieval literature, and she was looking forward to putting in a movie about Geoffrey Chaucer's *Canterbury Tales* and taking a nap.

On her way to class the phone band on her left arm vibrated. It was a text from Anthony, asking what time she would be home so he could drop off the dog. She started to type her simple reply "5ish" when she tripped over a student who had been bent over in the hallway tying his shoelaces. She managed to tuck and roll but the fall launched her digiTeacher Controller down the hallway, right at the feet of principal Sanjay Repalle, who was standing just outside her classroom door.

"Walking and texting is forbidden in the hallways for a reason, Miss Newton, even for faculty," he announced. He was a tall, dark ash-skinned Indian man with big brown eyes and no hair. He had a regal appearance that reminded her of a senator, and right now he looked very intimidating as he loomed over her rumpled figure lying on the hallway floor.

The poor student she had tripped over was kind enough to help her up as she apologized for not paying attention. He ran away quickly afterwards, not wanting anything to do with the situation that seemed to be unfolding with the faculty.

Principal Repalle picked up Catherine's digiTeacher Controller and inspected it, saying, "These controllers are very expensive, my dear. Please try to be more careful. Thankfully, this one appears to remain undamaged at present."

"I'm sorry, sir. I will try to be more careful," she said as she looked down at her vibrating phone band and cleared the screen quickly; Anthony had just sent a funny picture of Rufus's tongue licking the screen, with his eyes so wide you could see the whites at the top and bottom. *Did he put peanut butter on the screen?*

"Please see me after class, Miss Newton. I would like to discuss how you are doing here so far. Good day," he declared as he walked off into the crowd of students parting like the Red Sea all around him as if he were Moses. The way he said "Good Day" always seemed like some sort of commandment; she almost wanted to click her heels together and give him a salute. Or bow to him like he was a king. He sure ran this place like he was king.

Even as a teacher it never felt good to be called into the principal's office. Especially a principal that just caught you texting and walking over students. She was not having a good day. Thankfully, the fall was on her right side and her phone band was okay. She let

Anthony know she was going to be home closer to 6 now that she had to meet with the principal. He texted back with "lol badass." He was definitely a bad influence. That picture of Rufus was hilarious though. She looked at it again three more times throughout the day.

After the nap in medieval literature, she got a second wind and was able to make it the rest of the day without further incident. She did spend the entire afternoon dreading meeting with the principal though. *How bad could it be, really?* she thought. Besides assaulting her fellow teacher, Jordan, with a door the other day, and the texting and walking today, she was a model teacher. Well, unless you counted all the times she came in late through the back door. *He didn't know about that? Right? Oh man, she was a terrible teacher!*

The closer the time came to the final class ending, the more anxious she was getting. By the time the closing bell rang, she was so anxious she jumped in her seat at the sound. She heard muffled laughter from the class as she dropped her digiTeacher Controller on her desk and let out a pitiful, squeaky noise. It was time to head to the principal's office, to meet her fate. *Would she be re-assigned?*

Mr. Repalle's receptionist was busy typing up what she could only imagine was demerit letters to parents when Catherine walked into the administrative lobby. The receptionist, Mary Kingsley, was a short, chubby woman in her mid-fifties who looked like Shirley Temple, with a wide grin and a head full of curls. "Ah, we've been expecting you, Miss Newton," she said with a warm smile. "Go right on in, dear. He doesn't bite."

"Thank you, Mrs. Kingsley. What a lovely dress you are wearing," Catherine replied, trying to stall going into the office. "Are those flower blossoms on the hem?"

"Thank you, dear," she said as she sat up to show the tiny sunflowers along the edges of the skirt. "I always wear yellow on Fridays. It's the cheeriest color for the best day of the week," she added, then whispered, "Its okay, go on in." Mrs. Kingsley had seen right through her stalling efforts. She was probably used to everyone being scared of the principal.

Catherine straightened her back, brushed off her skirt and walked right up to the principal at his desk and said, "Good afternoon, Mr. Repalle" a little too loudly, as he looked up somewhat startled.

"My lovely, Miss Newton. Thank you for coming. Please, have a seat," he said as he put down his digital notebook, likely the principal's version of the digiTeacher Controller that she had been given on her first day of school. She wondered what he could do with his controller. Probably everything from sound an alarm at the school to rate the faculty on their performance. He sat back in his chair and said, "I realized today in the hallway that I haven't spoken to you since you arrived in August at the beginning of the school year. I know this is your first assignment and you have no family, so it must be lonely for you here in Desert Grande. I hope you are adjusting well to the desert and to the life of a school teacher?"

"Yes, sir. All of the students are great," she lied. *What was she supposed to say? The students were either annoying slackers or overachieving workaholics.* "I even have a silver level merit achiever in my homeroom. As far as adjusting to life in the desert, I am almost used to all the quakes now. I hardly notice them, except the big ones of course, like the one we had the other day."

"Ah, I forget the mine does make quite the impression on those who are not from here. It was unfortunate about your student Jonny Ricker falling and hitting his head in class during the last quake. The janitor said there had been a trail of blood from your homeroom to the nurse's office. That is why it is important for the students to remain seated during class, Miss Newton."

"Yes, sir. It won't happen again, sir, I promise," said Catherine quickly. She had forgotten about the sitting rule.

"Please, you do not have to call me sir, Miss Newton. I just want what is best for my faculty and staff, and all rules are there for a reason. We must maintain our integrity. We are the pillar of the community after all, the central rock on which this small mining town stands. I am a bit worried about you though. You look like you haven't slept in days. Is the workload too much?" he asked with genuine concern in his voice.

"No sir, I mean, Mr. Repalle. I just had trouble getting to sleep last night."

"Are you having nightmares?" he asked, suddenly leaning forward and very curious.

She was taken a little back by the question. "Actually, I have been having some weird dreams since I got here. You would think I was crazy if I told you," she said with a little uncomfortable laugh. *What sane person dreams of cyborgs?*

"This is a safe space, Miss Newton. You can tell me anything," he said earnestly.

Catherine seriously doubted that she could tell him anything, and was starting to wonder if that controller of his could send faculty to the mental hospital as well.

"Well, I keep having dreams where this man tells me to 'stop the mining'," Catherine replied, leaving out the part about the man being mechanically enhanced.

"Why does he want you to stop the mining?" he asked, looking at her intently.

"He won't tell me why the mining needs to stop. He will say just that it is getting more dangerous. Last time he said that the mining needs to stop or it will wake him, or worse, his brother."

"Wake him and his brother, you say? Hmmm ..." He sat back in his chair in contemplation. "So, it sounds to me that maybe your subconscious is not happy with all the quakes and this is interrupting your sleep. I can understand the quakes can be disturbing if you aren't used to them. Rest assured, Miss Newton, there is nothing to worry about. I've been here for over 15 years, ever since the mining company first got here. My brother Alluri owns Greggo Sands and our family was assigned here when he came to open the mine. The quakes have intensified in the last few years. I am not sure what they are up to in order to warrant such a big blast as they had Wednesday. I can see how that could be disturbing. Jonny wasn't the only one knocked down, and I have had complaints from other faculty members as well. I am sorry you are losing sleep. My brother has great respect for human life and works diligently to ensure the mining is done in a safe and professional manner. Unfortunately, quakes and tunnel failures are unavoidable. At least you can rest assured that there will be no quakes this weekend; the mine is closed for Josh Armstrong's father, Larry. He died in a collapsed corridor yesterday. Are you aware? It was a tragedy."

"Yes, I am aware. It is very sad. I heard he had three children. I didn't see Josh in class today, and I expect he will be out for a while. I think the funeral is this Sunday," Catherine said.

"Yes, I plan to be there. Will you be attending, Miss Newton?" he asked.

"Regrettably, I have other obligations so I won't be able to attend," she replied but immediately felt callous and followed up with, "How safe is the mine? I mean, this kind of thing doesn't happen very often, does it?"

"This tragedy is a rare occurrence indeed. But, I would not say the mine is a safe place no matter what my brother tries to assert," he paused for a minute, looking contemplative. "For instance, it is dangerous enough that one should not be wondering around the mine in the middle of the night. I hope you keep that in mind, Miss Newton," he said, pointedly and sternly, leaning forward for emphasis. Once he could see the shock register in her eyes that she realized he knew she had been in the mine last night, he stopped staring so hard and leaned back once again. "I am glad we were able to talk today, Miss Newton. Please, enjoy your weekend and I hope you get some rest. Feel free to come by my office anytime .... during the day. Good day."

As Catherine walked out of the room, a chill went down her spine. *How did he know she was at the mine in the middle of the night? Did Jordan tell him?* She walked in thinking he was going to re-assign her, only to get chastised for not getting enough sleep because she was wondering around the mine in the middle of the night. *Did everyone know everything about everyone in this small town?* It was a small world if the principal was the brother of the owner of the mine. She had mistakenly assumed the owner had to be someone named Greggo given the name. *Maybe Greggo Sands was a place? Another mine?*

There were two things she did know when she got into her car to head home. One, she was going to sleep unquestionably well tonight. Two, that thank God it was Friday! *Woo, hoo weekend!*

CHAPTER 4

Take a Hike

The weekend was going by too quickly. The days were getting colder so her hikes with her dog were getting shorter. Today, however, it felt extra-long because she had two dogs. Sass and Rufus where quite the pair. Sass was beautiful, elegant and a lady as she pranced along the trail right next to Catherine. Rufus was a half-black, half-white mix of fat fluffy shepherd. He was as distracted as a dog could get. He pulled ahead, weaving left and right along the trail, sniffing everything and everyone in sight. Catherine was getting bigger calves from digging in to hold Rufus back. Sass seemed amused.

Whenever a stranger would come up, Rufus was all over them, super friendly. He would jump up and lick them from head to toe, probably looking for crumbs of food. Sass would growl at anyone who came near her, super unfriendly. People had no idea how to react to the mix of the two dog's responses; neither was good. Rufus was large enough to knock over a full-grown man in his attempt to find food and Catherine constantly had to warn people not to try to pet Sass or she would bite. So, Catherine tended to look for less populated trails to avoid running into people when she hiked with both dogs.

Desert Grande had plenty of trails all throughout the valley and mountainside to choose from. Today,

Catherine decided to hike in a forested area near the east red rock mountains that reminded her of Montana where she grew up. The red dirt and rock was still foreign, but the evergreen trees and shrubs were as similar to the northwest as it got here in the desert. She was able to find a small dirt trail that followed a creek leading off from the main trail that it seemed everyone wanted to take today. After a few minutes away from the main path she felt she could finally breathe easy and enjoy the fall day. There were pink flowers on some of the bushes that were losing their petals. Their shades of pastel mixed with the grey and red rocks in the creek as they fell and drifted by.

She found a large log that cut across the creek like a tiny bridge and had mushrooms growing all along the sides. She sat on the log, inspecting the little mushrooms and let the dogs sip from the creek. She took off her shoes and socks and then let her tired feet cool in the stream. She couldn't help but feel at peace listening to the water trickle along the rocks and the rustle of little critters in the woods, splashing her toes to make ripples in the water.

Every now and then a raven would squawk, eliciting a small barking rampage from Rufus. Sass jumped up on the log and laid her head on Catherine's lap; she seemed to share in her contentment. Rufus jumped on the log and sniffed at the little mushrooms though didn't seem to find them appealing enough to eat. *Thank God!* she thought as she tried to imagine wrestling with Rufus over questionable mushrooms.

Catherine felt like she could sit on the log forever, but it was getting late. As she was putting her shoes and socks back on she could hear footsteps approaching. Sass was up and looking straight behind her, growling. Rufus almost jerked her backwards into the creek as he lunged towards the other side of the trail, in the opposite direction from where they had come. Someone was coming from deep in the woods.

As Catherine attempted to rein Rufus in, she saw the origin of the footsteps, a tall man in a jacket with the hood covering his face. He walked fast, with what looked like purpose. He seemed familiar.

"Jordan?" she blurted out.

"Catherine? How did you recognize me?" Jordan said as he pulled back the hood of his jacket. He walked closer to where she was sitting with the two dogs on the log.

"It was your walk. It is very distinctive. You're always looking like you are headed in a beeline straight for something important," she answered.

"I see. What are you doing out in the middle of the woods at dusk?" he asked as he tried, unsuccessfully, to not be knocked over and licked from head to toe by Rufus. He barely missed falling into the creek.

"As you can see, it is hard to keep Rufus off of people and the main path was a bit crowded today. I took a detour because I just needed some peace and quiet, and my arm needed a rest from wrestling Rufus off of people," she said as she pulled Rufus off of Jordan. "What about you? You look like you are up to no good with that hood up, all alone in the woods."

"I *am* up to no good," he replied with a smile. "I was just at the lake. It is about 2 miles north of here."

"What were you doing at the lake? Trying to catch a virus so you could get out of class?" she inquired as she pulled out some treats from her backpack to give to the dogs. "Did you see any mosquitos?"

"It is too cold for mosquitos. The whole virus thing is a lie anyway, and I am going to prove it. I know Greggo Sands is up to something; they have people all around the lake right now," he stated.

"What do you mean they have people all around the lake?" she said, puzzled.

"I mean, I saw people in white suits and masks, carrying what looked like test equipment, walking up and down the lake, looking for something. The suits had the Greggo Sands symbol on the sleeves. You do realize the lake has a direct run-off from the mines? I think they spilled something into the water and are trying to clean it up," he proclaimed.

"Why make up a story about viruses then? Why not just come out and say 'Hey, we spilled something, stay away from the lake while we clean it up'?" Catherine pointed out.

"The whole town relies on the mines, without the jobs that the company brings there would be no town. If the mines were implicated in the deaths of anyone who went to the lake they would have to close the mine for investigation and that could cost the whole town," he answered.

"But no one has died, right? I mean, none of the viruses are deadly from what I hear. They just cause strange reactions, like black scars on your skin or red welts or something, right?" Catherine said. Jordan was looking confused, and sullen as he sat on the log next to her. "I have only been here six months, so I might be missing something," she added, somewhat to console him.

"You are right. But, there is no mistaking what I saw. Plus, how does mining for viruses make any more sense than covering up toxic waste? You can't mine a virus, Catherine. The company is obviously cleaning something up at the lake," he insisted. "I am going to figure this out if it is the last thing I do."

"You know, there is something I want to figure out myself. How did Principal Repalle know I went to the mines the other day? Did you tell him, Jordan?" she asked, crossing her arms in disapproval.

Jordan countered with, "What do you mean he knew you went to the mines? Why in the world would anyone tell the brother of the owner of the mine that you were parading about looking in the tunnels while no one was there?"

"That's the thing, I didn't tell him. He showed up outside of my classroom right after I talked to you at lunch on Friday and asked me to meet him in his office at the end of the day. I thought he was going to reprimand me for hitting you with that door and that maybe he found out about all the times I have been showing up late. I was convinced I would be re-assigned but instead he gave me this speech about caring how I am doing, etc. ... and then ended it with a warning to not wander around the mine in the middle of the night!"

"Well, I didn't tell him," he replied. He paused for a minute, looking at Catherine without expression, then continued with, "You, perhaps, should not have told me either. What were you doing, anyway?"

"I wanted to see something. See, I had had this dream ..." She stopped herself. Was she actually going to tell him about her strange dreams? She didn't want him to think she was crazy. "It is getting late, we had better head back. I didn't bring a flashlight," she said as she got up from the log and crossed over the creek to the dirt trail.

"I see, a dream led you to stroll through dangerous tunnels all alone," he said as he followed behind her on the trail.

"I wasn't alone. I was with my boyfriend, Anthony."

"Oh yes, the famously handsome miner who loves to hunt," he said.

"Famously handsome?" she laughed.

"Isn't that what Elisabeth says?"

"Well, he is probably the most handsome man I have ever seen, but looks aren't everything you know."

"What is more important than looks?"

"Well, for one, having things in common is pretty important. Communication is a big one too. And great chemistry, of course," she said. She was starting to feel a little uncomfortable talking about this with Jordan. She hardly knew him, and what she knew about him so far is that he was paranoid and sullen, not the best traits in a person.

Rufus must have seen a squirrel, because he decided to try and rip Catherine's arm off to get to a nearby tree. Catherine liked her arm, so she let go of the rein in time to save it but not in time to stop from falling flat on her face in a pile of muddy leaves. Jordan was right beside her in a flash, helping her sit up and then heading over to go get Rufus from the tree. She sat on the trail, picking the leaves out of her hair, and spitting the mud from her mouth. Jordan was grappling with Rufus, trying to get him away from the tree that the squirrel had run up. Sass came over and started to lick Catherine's face. Jordan managed to calm Rufus down and lead him back over to where Catherine was sitting, still a bit dazed.

"You've got a small cut on your cheek. I've got some Neosporin and Band-Aids," Jordan declared as he removed his backpack to pull out a first aid kit, a small cloth and some water. He drenched the cloth in water and started to wipe her face clean. "I guess we are both clumsy when we are distracted," he said with a smile.

"Ha! Yeah, I can hardly see the welt on your head anymore," she replied as she brushed his hair off his forehead to check out the bruising from his encounter with the nurse's office door windowpane. There were flakes of gold in his brown eyes that she never noticed before, and his lips seemed so soft. She could feel her heart starting to beat faster and her body began to feel warm all over. As he applied the Neosporin his fingers lightly grazed her cheek and she felt flutters in her stomach. *Wow, talk about chemistry!* She blushed as the thought entered her head and turned away from Jordan to see Sass looking at her sideways.

"Umm, ah, so, Anthony, that's my boyfriend, left his phone band at the mine and we went to go get it because he couldn't live without it over the weekend. That's why I was at the mine in the middle of the night, rescuing my boyfriend's phone," she declared.

"I see," he said as he applied the band-aid and offered a hand to help Catherine to her feet.

"Yes, I came along for the adventure," she said as she put her hand in his hand. He pulled her up and she stumbled forward into his chest. Her heart was beating so fast she could hear it thudding in her ears. She was in his arms, looking up into his golden-brown eyes that were drawing her in like deep, unexplored caves. He was looking down at her, expressionless, dead still. Her heart skipped a beat as he leaned forward to remove another leaf from her hair.

"So, you are an adventurer?" he asked. "What did this adventure into a mine have to do with a dream?"

Catherine pulled away. What could she say? How to begin? "I have a lot of dreams, vivid dreams. I always have, ever since I was a little girl," she answered while fidgeting.

"And you dreamt about going into the mines at night?" he inquired.

"No. Remember Wednesday, when that huge blast went off?" she said as she started to walk along the trail. She still wasn't sure if she should be saying what she was saying, but now that she was saying it she might as well continue.

"Yeah, the day you hit me with the door, how could I forget?" he said as he followed behind her along the trail.

"Well, that night I had a dream. There was a man, I've seen him in a few dreams actually, and he always tells me to 'Stop the mining'. Like I can stop the mining, right? Anyway, that night he said they found one of his labs. The next day when Anthony was telling me about his day, he mentioned they had come across something that looked like a lab. His supervisor told him it was an old Navajo tunnel though. I know it sounds crazy but I just wanted to see it for myself. It seemed like such a weird coincidence, you know?"

"From what I recall, the Navajo did not have tunnels in this area; they weren't a tunneling people. I can do a little research on the area though, just to make sure," Jordan responded. After a brief silence, he said, "What did your boyfriend think of the dream?"

"I didn't tell him, I just said I was curious about the lab," she replied.

"I see," he stated as he walked on the trail behind Catherine. "Did the man say anything else in the dream?"

"Yeah, he said that the mining was dangerous and that it might wake him, or worse, his brother," she said. "I know, I sound crazy."

"Well, it is just a dream," he replied. He walked for a few seconds, then added: "It does seem odd that he is telling you that he is asleep in a dream."

"What do you mean? He was awake and taking to me in my dream," she responded.

"No, he said not to wake him, which meant he was asleep and so was his brother," he pointed out.

"Great, now I am super wacky, dreaming about sleep-walking cyborgs!" she exclaimed.

"Wait, what? You never mentioned he was a cyborg," he said while laughing. "So, you are dreaming of a dreaming cyborg? Is his brother a cyborg too?"

"Yeah, I have very vivid and weird dreams. Now you think I am insane for sure," she said, cringing.

"No, it was just a dream. I wouldn't worry about it, really," he laughed, then added: "I do wonder why you didn't tell your boyfriend about it though. How serious is the relationship anyway?"

"Pretty serious, I think. He's Catholic and wants a big family right away. I swear, last time I visited his sister she tried to measure me for a wedding gown!" she proclaimed as she stopped on the trail and turned to see how Jordan was doing handling Rufus. He had both hands on the reins and was still being dragged through the mud.

"You don't sound too happy about that. Do you not want to get married?" he inquired as he looked up from Rufus long enough to almost be dragged down.

"I don't know. It is all so fast. We have only been dating for four months and we haven't even ..." she was about to say 'had sex' when she cut herself off. That was more than he needed to know. *Wow, was she just going to tell him everything that popped into her head today?*

"Haven't even what?" he asked, looking perplexed.

Catherine was trying to think of something fast. "We haven't even gone camping yet," she stated. That was all she could think of, she wasn't a very good liar. *Camping?*

"Yes, a good camping trip can certainly tell you a lot about a person," he said with a laugh.

"You sure do laugh a lot more when you aren't at school," she declared as she continued walking down the trail.

"Well, I have to keep appearances or those students wouldn't be afraid of me anymore. A stern look of authority, with severe gravity keeps them in line," he stated with the firmest face and voice possible. It was disturbing. He obviously had years of practice.

They were at the parking lot off the main trail already. *How did they get there so fast?* Catherine wondered.

"My car is that way," she said, pointing left.

"My car is that way," he said, and pointed in the opposite direction. "I guess this is goodbye. Let me know if you want someone to go 'camping' with, my schedule is pretty open," he professed as he took her hand, gave it a gentle kiss and then placed the reins to Rufus in her palm.

He was walking away before she could open her mouth to try and respond. It was probably a good thing too because she had no idea what to say. He had guessed what 'camping' meant, and when his soft, warm lips had touched her hand she knew the chemistry was unmistakable because the fluttering in her stomach and the flushing of her skin went off in coordination. She began to wonder about how Italian he was. His last name was Muntz, so he had to be somewhat German. Most of the time he had that expressionless, yet superior German attitude when he was at school. But that smile, and those eyes. They conveyed so much passion it was almost overwhelming. Her roommate in college had dated an Italian guy; he was passionate indeed!

Catherine had to shake herself to some sense. Nothing was ever going to happen between her and Jordan. Anthony was her man, and even though they had never had sex, she was sure there would be plenty of chemistry when they did, based on all the heated make-out sessions that they had shared so far. The last thing she needed right now is another guy confusing her feelings for Anthony; they were already confused enough as it was.

She got the dogs in the car and sat back while the autopilot took her home. She spent the car ride home looking in the mirror as she removed debris from her hair and cleaned the mud off her neck and ears where Sass and Jordan had missed.

When she got to the house she could see Anthony's car in the driveway. He wasn't due back until tomorrow. Rufus saw the car too and started jumping and going berserk to get out. As soon as she opened her car door, he ran right to the other car and jumped at the door. Anthony must have been sleeping in the car because he sprang up and opened the door.

"Hey, Babe! I thought you were going to be out all weekend?" Catherine questioned as she walked up to the car. "Is everything all right?"

"Yes," he replied as he gave her a firm kiss and hug. "We managed to get three Elk in one day! That was all we were licensed to get this season, so we were a bit too successful. Man, I managed to shoot a 7-point buck with one arrow! Rodge was pissed because his buck was only a 5-pointer. Steven got a 4-pointer. Three bucks in one day and those guys are whining about not getting to put that 7-pointer in their living room, like we could share. Ha!"

"Should I be expecting an elk stew anytime soon?" she asked.

"No, we usually just keep the racks and heads for trophies and sell the meat. Rodge already brought the bulls down to the butcher this afternoon. Elk stew does sound good though. I haven't had anything since lunch. I came straight here after I went home to shower. I was hoping to surprise you. Oh wait," he said as he reached into the car. He pulled out a bouquet of wildflowers. "I found a whole field of flowers when we were out hunting, I figured you might like them."

"They are beautiful, Anthony. Thank you!" she exclaimed as she gave him another kiss. "Let's go inside and I can see what you might like from the combinator." With that they headed inside. She removed her coat and gloves and placed them on the hanger in the entryway. She filled two bowls each of food and water for the dogs and then looked up her phone band to check the combinator options for the humans. She lifted the band from her arm and pressed the button to straighten it for holding out in front of them so Anthony could look at the options too.

"Let's see, we could have tuna casserole or chicken lasagna. That seems to be about it for two people. There is enough Salisbury steak for one though. I usually do my shopping on Sundays, so we are a bit short on options. If you want, I could order Salisbury steak for you and when that is done I could have tuna casserole," she offered.

"Okay, that sounds like a good plan. Salisbury steak it is," he proclaimed as he gave her a kiss on the forehead. She placed the order in the app on her phone band.

"What happened to your face?" he asked as he touched the band-aid on her cheek.

"Oh, Rufus tried to catch a squirrel. He and the squirrel were fast, I was slow. I ended up face down in the mud," she replied. "Speaking of mud, I wouldn't mind taking a shower. Can you watch the dogs? Sometimes they fight over food when Rufus finishes before Sass and he is still hungry."

"Sure, Babe, no problem," he answered as he learned back and turned on the south wall to ESPN.

As Catherine washed off the mud and twigs from her hair, she kept going over the conversation she had with Jordan in her head. *Why did she just blurt out everything in front of him, with no filter? Maybe because it felt like she could tell him anything and he wouldn't judge her?* She had told him so much already. *Why couldn't she talk to Anthony like that? Maybe she should just try harder to open up to Anthony? Maybe she could start with telling him about her dreams and see what he would say? That's it. It was decided!* She would tell him about her dreams tonight.

Catherine got dressed in a light blue silk shorts and tank-top nighty and went downstairs. Anthony had already started munching on his Salisbury steak and potatoes. Rufus was sitting at his feet drooling and begging for pieces from his plate. Sass was curled up in her bed in the corner.

"Yes! Go, Go, Go!!" Anthony yelled as he jumped up from his seat, fork flinging potatoes that Rufus was more than happy to clean up. Catherine looked over to see a man running with a football get taken down by three other men.

"Did he make a touchdown?" she asked, trying to sound like she cared. She really wasn't a football fan, but every guy she had ever met was a fan.

"Almost. Sourier caught an interception and ran for 40 yards, now the Buffaloes have the ball," he exclaimed, not looking away from the screen the entire time he talked. He sat back down, still so completely engrossed that he wasn't even looking at the food he was scooping into his mouth. It looked like they would be watching the game tonight.

Catherine walked over to the combinator in the kitchen. Anthony had left the door open so her tuna casserole hadn't started yet. She shut the door and then went back to the entryway to pick up the dog bowls to put in the dishwasher. She set the Rhomba to clean up the mess around the doorway where the dog bowls had been. They must have fought a little over the food because it was everywhere. She then picked up her hiking shoes next to the door. She looked for Anthony's shoes and realized he never took them off. They were on his feet, which were on the coffee table. She went over to him and took off his shoes, trying to avoid breathing due to the smell of his feet. *Didn't he say he just took a shower?* she thought. She set the shoes by the entryway in the shoe cleaner hatch and then took the wildflowers he had brought her into the kitchen to find a vase. She placed the flowers in the vase on the coffee table next to his feet. She was hoping the proximity would help hide the smell. She then sat down and cuddled on the couch next to Anthony. *Maybe they could make out during commercials?*

"Do you want me to stay the night?" he asked, looking down on her curled up next to him. "I can control myself if you can. I have never slept with a woman before. I think it would be great to cuddle like this all night long, don't you?"

"I would love that," she said. It was an exciting thought, though she wasn't sure if she could control herself. She had never just "slept" with a man before either. It would give her more time to try and talk to him. Right now, he was so engrossed in the game it was impossible to say more than a sentence or two.

When the game finished she took him by the hand and led him upstairs to the bedroom. Her alarm was a digital projection on the ceiling that tracked time and weather conditions as images floating by as sunshine, clouds, rain, a starry sky, etc. She could set it to real time weather, or select another option or sky pattern. She even had Hubble telescope images to choose from, which were her favorite. They lay there for a few minutes looking up at a starry sky representing the current conditions, with little meteors that passed once a minute. He laid her head on his chest and then he put his arms around her, pulling her close to his side.

Ok, if you're going to talk, talk now! she thought. "Do you have any strange dreams, Anthony?" she inquired, thinking the question was a good transition to talking about her dreams.

"No, I never dream, or I never remember them anyway" he declared. "I mean I have dreams like goals and things I want for my life. Like a family, kids, you know. I've told you this stuff before. Definitely nothing 'strange.' I want to be a good father, teach my kids about mining, geology, hunting. Even if I have daughters, I want them to hunt too. Be good with a bow and arrow like their dad, you know? Man, a 7-point buck! That was a nice one, I am looking forward to mounting that in my living room!"

Catherine could imagine Anthony being a great dad. She could picture their kids running around, adorable and adventurous, hunting in the woods. As she was distracted, thinking about kids, she heard a rumbling growling. The growling turned into a spurt of snorts, followed by what could have passed for a chainsaw. It was shocking; it was coming from Anthony! He was snoring, and it was loud! This was something he should have warned her about because she didn't have any earplugs. He also had a tight grip on her with his arm around her, holding her oh so close to the gaping source of the cacophony. She couldn't pry herself loose; she was stuck! She lay there, miserably awake, wondering what in the world she had done in her life to make her deserve to be tortured by a wailing gargoyle throughout the night.

CHAPTER 5

Just a Day at the Job

Anthony was a humble man who wanted a modest life. He knew he was not the smartest man and he never intended or even thought to go to college. He got a job directly out of high school working in the mine to support his family. His favorite part about the job was blowing things up, that's why he signed up to be a blast helper from the start. What he lacked in book smarts, he made up for in street smarts and leadership skills. He was able to work his way to crew lead in just a few years and he was on track to be the next foreman. If he was going to do a job, he was going to do it well.

He always strove to do what was right by his family and for God. He began each day with a prayer, thanking God for his blessings. Today, he made sure to thank God for Catherine and allowing a night with her without falling for temptation. Holding her in his arms, he felt complete. He had fallen asleep so quickly when he spent the night at her place this past Saturday. It was probably the best sleep of his life.

He felt they were very compatible. She had the book smarts to his street smarts. She reminded him of a teacher he had had a crush on when he was 12. He loved how great she was with kids too because he planned to have at least six.

His whole family was pushing him to marry Catherine, convinced she would convert to Catholicism as soon as they were engaged. He didn't need much convincing; he had fallen for Catherine from the start. Ariana, his youngest sister, helped him pick out a ring this past Sunday. Gretchen, the second youngest sister, had aspirations to be their wedding planner and had already tried to measure Catherine for a wedding dress when she wasn't paying attention. His parents were thrilled and couldn't wait for grandchildren.

This next Thursday, on their weekly date night, Anthony was planning to propose to Catherine. He had to come up with a good spot, and he was still trying to work out the words to say. He was excited, and ready for the next step in his life. Everything was coming together for him and he could hardly sit still with anticipation.

Monday morning work went by in a flash as his team dug further down Tunnel One where the corridor collapsed last Thursday on Larry's crew. They were putting in extra supports today to ensure no further collapse, and Foreman Gamble came by to inspect the work himself. When Anthony went back to the washing station to clean up for lunch, Foreman Gamble pulled him aside and asked if he would meet him in his office when he was done eating.

Anthony had no clue what the meeting was for, and he didn't stress about it either: he would find out soon enough. *Maybe he was looking to fill Larry's position already?* That would be a promotion with training. He put it out of his mind for the time being. He was starving and looking forward to reminding Rodge and Steven about the buck shoot this weekend during lunch. They were already in the cafeteria showing pictures to a couple of the other guys from their crew when Anthony came in.

"Hey Rodge, you tell them I brought down that 7-pointer with only one arrow?" Anthony asked as he sat down next to Steven, who was chowing down on some beef stew. Steven and Rodge were both a couple of years younger than Anthony, and had joined his crew two years ago. They had all hit it off instantly and had been inseparable ever since.

"Yeah, you know I let you have that one. I pointed him out to you and the next thing I know, you were up and shooting. You spooked the whole herd and if we hadn't happened across that second gang then both Steven and I would have been pissed and you know it," Rodge declared. Rodger Lombardi was a short, dark Italian with a hooked nose. He had a little bit of a gut and an attitude big enough to make up for his small stature.

"You pointed him out? Ha!" Anthony laughed. "Yeah, right! I was locked on him before you said anything and you know it. It was your arm movement that spooked him, that's why I had to take the shot right then. Isn't that right, Steven?"

"Huh? What?" Steven said, looking perplexed and annoyed. "You know I wasn't looking, we've been over this already," Steven urged, between mouthfuls of stew. "We caught 3 bucks in one day, that's amazing! Who can say that? Who cares who saw the first buck, let it go! We all went home with good trophies for the season."

Steven Chan was very tall and thin, despite his veracious appetite. He was half-Chinese and half-Irish, with green slanted eyes and a few little freckles on his cheeks. He usually had the most sense of the trio despite being the youngest.

"It matters because I get to take home a sweet rack to mount on my wall, right above my fireplace," Anthony gloated. "You are taking good care of my trophy, aren't you, Rodge?"

"What kind of guy do you think I am, man? I brought all three by the taxidermist this morning. He said they should be ready in a few weeks," replied Rodge. "Speaking of trophies, how's that hot little teacher of yours? She like those flowers you, so delicately, picked for her?"

"At least I have a girlfriend. Maybe you should think about taking a shower every now and then, Rodge. The circling flies might decide to leave you alone long enough for a girl to see you," Anthony responded, jokingly.

Anthony finished off his stew, wiping the bowl with the last of his cornbread and gulping it down in one bite. "I've gotta run. Boss man says he wants to meet with me."

"What's old Gamble want with you?" Rodge asked.

"You thinking he wants to promote you? Maybe give you Larry's job?" Steven asked.

"I don't know, but he sure didn't want to meet with you two losers so I guess it is a promotion," Anthony said as he smacked Steven on the back. "I'm headed out to the shed. Don't do anything stupid while I'm gone."

The shed is what they called the three-story, cement office where all the bosses, finance and HR spent most of their day. All their desks were set along the perimeter of each floor, facing inward with glass separating the offices from the center. There were several working elevators in the center, each marked by a circle on the ground. When someone on an elevator was about to enter the floor, the ground would light up and buzz. If there was an object or person on top of the circle, the floor wouldn't open. Else, it would open and whatever was above or below would be moved using a clear tube into the circular area. Then the tube would leave and it would just be the person standing there. The tubes utilized a pressurized vacuum system that was highly efficient and very fast, even with large objects. In the very center of the room was a giant pillar. The pillar had various news stations projecting on all four sides. Above and below the stations were live feeds from cameras planted within the mines. The floor was 15- feet tall, and every three feet, on each of the four sides, there was a live display. The displays and stations would change and rotate periodically.

The first time Anthony had been to the shed was also the last time he had been there: when he was initially hired into the company over four years ago. He had forgotten how fast everyone walked, moved and talked in the shed. The constant flashing of the projections in the center and the movement of the tubes whistling by was a whirlwind, and he couldn't image anyone being able to get anything done with that distraction.

Gamble walked out of the office three cubicles up to the left and waved Anthony over. Anthony walked forward, slowly, keeping close to the glass and as far away from the elevator tubes as possible. The constant movement in the center gave him a little vertigo. Even from where he was standing he could feel the air move as people went through the tubes. He didn't want to get any closer for fear of being sucked down a tube.

"Anthony, I am sure you know why I asked you to come to my office today," Gamble stated, simply, as he crossed his hands on his lap and sat back in his seat. He was a stout but firm man, with steel blue eyes and freckles almost covering his face. His thinning auburn hair was missing from the front half of his head, which shone with beads of sweat.

"I'm sorry sir, but I have no idea," Anthony replied, honestly. He gingerly took a seat in the chair across from Gamble at the large office table. The table was fully topped with pictures of his family, a large black briefcase, a collection of rocks from the mine as well as three computer monitors.

"Did you think we wouldn't find out? We have cameras everywhere. Even when we are shut down, they continue to run. I should fire you, right here, right now," Frank Gamble threatened as he turned his right most monitor around to show two shadowy figures looking around a room with a flashlight. The image was dark and hard to discern, but when the man holding the flashlight looked up and pointed it at the ceiling, his face was clear as day on the camera for a brief second. It was Anthony, looking for those ventilation shafts in the middle of the room that he had thought might be a lab.

"What in the world made you want to do what looks like some kind of spy investigation, in my mine? I got heat from Mr. Repalle himself this morning. That whole area is closed off due to radiation. You realize that you and your little teacher girlfriend are lucky to be alive?" Foreman Gamble asked angrily. "What were you thinking, young man?"

"I was just trying to impress my girlfriend, honestly sir. I had only come in to get my phone band from my locker and she wanted to explore. I didn't realize there was a radiation leak, sir. If I had I wouldn't have gone down that corridor. She had never been in a mine before. She was curious and I ...." Anthony continued to explain but Frank was no longer looking in his direction, something on the other side of the glass wall had caught his attention. Anthony turned around to see what had caught his eye.

On the other side of the wall, an old gray-haired man with a large tool belt around his waist full of tools had appeared in one of the tubes. He had started to walk quickly towards the glass of Foreman Gamble's office and then he abruptly fell. There was blood coming from his eyes and ears and he was convulsing on the floor, coughing up blood. Several people had come out of their offices to see what was going on but Gamble bolted out and yelled at everyone to stay back. He pressed a few buttons on a small device at his waist and then told Anthony to go get the briefcase off of his desk. Once Anthony brought him the briefcase, he punched a few numbers into the control panel on the top and it opened. There was what appeared to be a hazmat suit inside the case on one side and on the other side were four injectors filled with differing colored fluids. In addition, there was also a small device inside that Foreman Gamble reached for first after putting on a pair of gloves and a mask. He then ran the device over the forehead of the old man. It kept beeping and turning red, but Gamble tried it over and over.

"This is not happening," Gamble whispered, closing his eyes. The old man had stopped convulsing and his empty eyes were staring straight up at the ceiling.

"What did you say?" Anthony asked as he moved in closer, leaning down towards the old man to see if he had a pulse.

"Everyone stay back!" Gamble yelled, pushing Anthony back and almost knocking him down.

Three of the circles lit up at once, several people had to take a step back towards their offices to make way for the elevator tubes. Men in hazmat suits appeared with briefcases similar to the one that Foreman Gamble had opened next to the man on the floor.

Foreman Gamble shook his head and said, "This one is new, check where he came from. We need to contain this, NOW!" He motioned towards Anthony and said, "Take this one too, he needs to be debriefed and quarantined."

Before Anthony knew what was happening, two of the men had him by the arms and were taking him down one of the tubes. All he could see was light whizzing by, he felt like he was going a million miles an hour and then he felt weightless as the tube decelerated to a smooth stop. It all happened in a matter of seconds. He was brought to a large room that looked like a prison center with nothing but 10-foot steel doors all around. He was placed in the room behind one of the huge doors and the men were gone before he could even speak.

Anthony turned around in a circle, taking in the room. It looked like a doctor's office inside. There was a locked cabinet with medical appliances, with a built-in sink that had a soap dispenser. There was a doctor's table and a small rotating chair. Anthony sat on the doctor's table and waited.

After what felt like an eternity, another man in a hazmat suit entered the room saying, "Hi, I'm Dr. Steinman. I believe you may have been exposed to something dangerous and I will need to examine you."

Dr. Steinman motioned towards the table and said, "Please have a seat." He then walked over to the locked cabinet and removed what looked like a long syringe. "This may sting a little," he said as he placed the needle in the back of Anthony's neck. There was a petite box on the bottom shelf of the cabinet in which the doctor placed a few drops from the needle. It beeped three times and a red light appeared on the top. The doctor quickly turned around and smiled. "It appears you are all clear. I will be right back."

With that, the doctor was out the door with the little black box in hand. About 15 minutes later, the door opened again but this time it was Foreman Frank Gamble that entered the small room. "I bet this is very confusing for you, Anthony, am I right?" he asked as he sat in the chair next to the cabinet.

"Yes sir. Will that old man be okay?" Anthony inquired.

"No. It seems that he has died of a stroke. It is never easy to see a fellow coworker die, even when they are

76-years-old and still trying to work like they are in their 20s," Foreman Gamble replied, mournfully.

"But, why the hazmat suits and why am I here if he was just having a stroke?" Anthony questioned, bewildered. None of this added up right.

"Listen, Anthony, I need to level with you. You do have a family, Anthony? Two sisters, a mother and an Aunt here, from what I remember, right? You wouldn't want anything to happen to your family, am I clear, Anthony?" Foreman Gamble asked, pointedly. "Here at the mine, we are all one big family. We're very protective of our own family too. We must all work to protect our family. You've been part of my crew for over four years now and today when you helped me with the briefcase and the old man it was another example of the quick thinking and hard work that has earned you crew lead status. Leadership, you know, is all about setting the example. Sometimes you do not have all the answers, but you have to do what is right for your family. Without the mines, this city would not exist. Our family, would dissolve. Again, I ask, you wouldn't want anything to happen to your family, would you, Anthony?"

"No, sir. My family is the most important thing to me, sir."

"Good. I am glad to hear that. Before your little investigation adventure with your girlfriend, I was considering you for training into Larry's position as lead blast engineer. Now, I am not sure if I can trust you. I need you to prove to me that I can trust you," Foreman Gamble insisted.

"I am willing to do whatever is necessary, sir," Anthony said, reflexively. He was still in shock.

"Good. For now, know that everything we have done today is to protect you, because you are family. I don't ask questions of leadership, and they have not explained anything to me and I am okay with that. I need you to be okay with that. Are we clear?" Foreman Gamble questioned.

"Yes sir," Anthony responded, knowing there was no other way to answer the question.

"Also, no more nighttime adventures in the corridors; it is not safe. Are we clear on that as well?"

"Of course, sir. It will never happen again," Anthony pleaded.

"Thank you. I will be keeping an eye on you, Anthony. Please do not make me regret my trust in you," Foreman Gamble insisted.

Gamble pressed a button on his waistband and it opened the steel door. He then led Anthony through the hallway and into one of the elevator tubes. The deceleration at the top made Anthony feel like his blood was being pulled into his feet and almost made him black out. When he could see clearly, he saw that he was face-to-face with the pillar of flashing news stations and video feeds at the center of the offices where he had been earlier. Everything seemed back to normal, people in their offices going about their day as if nothing happened.

"Now, get back to work," Gamble announced as he headed into his office and shut the glass door behind him.

Anthony was dumbstruck and walking in a daze as he headed back down to the mine. There was a long passageway along the cliff face that led from the shed to the mine. He stopped, and while holding onto the guardrail, he threw up his lunch over the side of the cliff. Down below he could see the clear blue lake that had been carved out by a glacier millions of years ago. The whole area seemed blissful and serene as a gentle breeze blew past and left sparkling ripples along the lake and set the trees in motion. Anthony wiped his mouth and continued forward towards the mine.

Family. The most important thing to Anthony was family and he was pretty sure Foreman Gamble had just threatened his family. He would do anything to protect his sisters, mother and aunt and that included keeping his mouth shut about everything that happened today. He didn't like to lie, it was against his religion, but not saying something was not the same as a lie. So, he planned to just forget about it and never bring it up. *That was the right thing to do, right?*

He stopped again on the bridge to say a prayer and ask God what to do. He stood there looking out at the mine and back to the shed. He stared at the lake below, and couldn't help but notice how peaceful the whole area was this time of day. He noticed a helicopter coming into the helipad, and Alluri Repalle, the mine owner himself, walked out to greet a group of men and women waiting for him near the shed entrance. Whatever was going on, it looked like they had everything under control and he had never heard of anything going on before now. This was all way above his pay grade.

That man was very old and really could have died of a stroke for all he knew; he had never seen anyone die of a stroke before. After what Anthony had done, getting caught snooping around the mine in the middle of the night, he felt lucky to still have a job. After what he saw today, he felt lucky to be alive. And, if he kept his mouth shut, he might just get that promotion after all.

By the time he got back to his shift, everyone was cleaning up to go home. He walked to the washing station and began to clean his hands. He noticed a small bunch of dark red dots that were coming off in the water in streaks. It must have been blood splattered from the old man when he was coughing and writhing on the floor. Anthony decided to use a little extra soap this time, just to be sure he got his hands clean.

"So, what did the Foreman want with you all afternoon?" Steven asked as he started to wash his hands next to Anthony.

"Yeah, you were gone all day. Man, you look pale, are you okay?" Rodge inquired with concern as he came up to the other side of Anthony at the washing station.

"Let's just say you might be looking at the next lead blast engineer," Anthony responded with as big of a smile as he could muster. That wasn't lying, Foreman Gamble did hint at him getting Larry's job.

"No way, man! That is awesome. Did you start training today? Is that why you were gone so long?" Steven asked.

"No, I haven't started training yet. We had a long discussion about leadership," Anthony responded. "And, we talked about how he didn't know anyone except me that could deal with you two lazy bozos that can't drill a blast hole to save your life."

"Is that so? Well, I'll have you know I drilled three blast holes without your supervision today, and they are perfect," replied Rodge.

"Perfectly uneven. Hector had to go through and ream the holes you drilled just to get the explosive pouches in," declared Steven.

"Oh, and yours were better?" Rodge retorted.

"Hey, I never said I was perfect! You're the one saying your crappy blast holes are perfect," Steven exclaimed as he shook his wet hands dry in Rodge's direction, splatting him in the face with hot water droplets. Rodge responded with flicking water at Steven from the running water, getting it on Anthony as well in the process.

"Children, please! See, this is what I was talking about, a couple of bozos," Anthony said as he took a towel off the rack and proceeded to twist it, then flick the end of it at the back of Rodge's rear end. Rodge jumped and almost landed in the washing station, then splashed water at Anthony's face in defense. Steven went for another towel off of the rack and Anthony battled him back.

They were interrupted when second shift started billowing into the washing room to get ready. Anthony dried off his arms and face with the towel he had been using to fight off Rodge and Steven. He noticed a little red come off from the back of his neck where the needle had gone into his skin. A chill went down his spine as he was suddenly reminded of the day's events. He threw the towel into the bin with the others and got his belongings out of his locker.

"Just another day at the mine, just another day at the mine" Anthony said aloud to himself as he got into his car to head home. He planned to forget everything he could about today.

CHAPTER 6

Boss Man

Alluri Repalle sat in his helicopter, looking over at the view below. The wilderness of America was magnificent: he could see a herd of horses playing in a river and red boulders all around shaped like ancient guardians of the wild. Sitting across from him, and deliberately not looking out the window, was his head of research and development in Russia, Sasha Mikhailov. Her knuckles were white from how hard she was clutching the briefcase on her lap. He asked how she was doing and she produced only a strained smile on her pale face. Apparently, she wasn't a fan of heights.

"Don't worry, you're perfectly safe," he said with as much authority as he could to try and ease her anxiety. He was used to having authority and responsibility from a young age. He was the third child, and second eldest son of 10 children in a highly prestigious Brahmin Hindu family. His father and mother had both filled various roles in politics back in India. He rarely saw his parents while he was growing up, and became very close to his siblings, helping to teach and raise them. He strove hard to be successful to show a good example, and to be seen as honorable in his parent's eyes. He came to America when he was 16 and he earned dual degrees in mechanical and metallurgical engineering from the Colorado School of

Mines. He followed those with an MBA from Harvard before becoming employed at the mining company Greggo Sands. After several quick promotions, he became the CEO and bought the majority share in the company so that he could run it exactly the way he saw fit.

Then the war came. The Great War of Dust they called it. Even though it lasted just a few short years, the aftermath of the radioactive dust across the planet left most areas uninhabitable. Five of his siblings and his father died in the war, two more died slowly just a few years after from the dust. Sickness and death was all around him for years, so he poured his devotion and energy into his work, expanding the mining company and investing in new research and technology.

When his eldest brother and mother took an assignment here over 15 years ago, he had no idea the mines in the area would end up being the crown jewel of his company. In fact, he didn't even know if they would produce anything of value. It was his brother Sanjay who persuaded him to invest more in the old mines, to support the build-up of the new community. Luckily, he found high levels of bauxite, which was a key ingredient for the energy harvesting ceramic roads his company had been developing over the last decade. But, what was discovered recently was much more valuable, and more dangerous.

Alluri stepped off the helicopter at the landing pad above the main governing building for the Desert Grande branch of Greggo Sands. He and Sasha were met by several members of his staff and then escorted down to the offices below. Sasha discretely headed straight down to the research floors below while Alluri made the rounds through the offices, greeting as much of the staff as he could. He found that the best way to keep track of what was going on in his company was to engage with employees at every level. Sometimes the lower level engineers and supervisors would let slip details that the upper managers tried to keep hidden from him because they did not want to let him know they didn't have control over absolutely everything.

"How is the expansion coming in Corridor One Mr. Gamble?" he said as he approached the office of the head foreman for the site, Frank Gamble, who was apprehensively waiting for him outside the door.

"Couldn't be better, we are making great progress now that we are back to work today. We're spending extra time reinforcing as we go to ensure no future collapse," replied Frank Gamble, shaking Alluri's hand with vigor. There was a sternness to this foreman that he always appreciated; it helped him keep a tight crew.

"Good," declared Repalle. Then he brought Frank a little closer and said soft enough for only him to hear, "And the little incident with the curious couple?"

"Nothing, just a young man trying to impress his girlfriend," whispered Frank sincerely, looking confident, though still shaking Alluri's hand.

"We've all been there, my friend, haven't we?" said Alluri as he patted Frank on the back, which seemed to cue Frank to finally release his hand. Women were more trouble than mines. His wife still expected rubies and diamonds whenever they got into an argument. That reminded him, he would have to get her a gold bangle just for taking this last-minute trip, with no notice, or he could expect grief when he got back that night.

He looked around for more employees to visit, giving Sasha more time below. There weren't many more offices on this floor, and it was getting close to the end of first shift. The head of HR was pregnant, and he wanted to make sure he congratulated her on the blessing of her second child before making his way down to the Research Department. He found her office across the tubes, and was able to pop in just as she was packing up to leave. Afterwards, he typed a code into his belt and the tube took him to where the real research was taking place, 10 stories down.

Sasha Mikhailov was there waiting for him in a glass enclosed inspection room. She and Dr. Steinman were in quarantine, in full gear, examining the body of the old man who had died earlier this afternoon. Alluri stood outside the lab looking through the glass and listening into the intercom for the full report.

"It is both miraculous and frightening, sir," said Sasha, with her strong Russian accent.

"Yes, it is unlike anything we have seen before," explained Dr. Steinman. "All other enhancements have been viral. So, when he tested negative, it was assumed he may have died of natural causes. That was until we were able to examine his brain. There was a residue covering most of the synaptic tissue. Upon examination it was found to be a neurotoxin excreted by an unknown, gram-positive bacterium."

Dr. Steinman walked over to a microscope, and turned around a computer monitor to show moving bacteria suspended in liquid as he said, "We have found traces of the bacteria in his blood. However, we found none on his clothes or body, nor in Tunnel Three where he had been working last week before we closed it down for radiation. It looks as if the bacteria survives for long periods of time, dormant, but it is not resistant to our high heat cleaning methods. So, most traces are probably destroyed. It was likely kept in the form of a fine powder in one of the glass containers that were shattered during the blast last Wednesday."

Sasha interrupted with, "It seems Mr. Grayson here was heading up the initial clean-up crew and came across some broken glass that he failed to mention." She lifted his right hand, which appeared to have a large cut. "He must have cleaned up all the evidence, fearing reprisal."

"A bacterial neurotoxin? Fascinating!" said Alluri. "Can we synthesize any for further testing from his blood? What does the excreted neurotoxin do exactly? How did it kill him?"

"From what we can tell, it enhances neural activity. His brain and nervous system must have been firing at exceptional rates right before he died, given the amount of damage we found. We are already synthesizing the neurotoxin and growing a culture of the bacteria for further testing," replied Dr. Steinman.

"This would be the first enhancement we have found to increase brain activity," Sasha quickly added.

"This is also the first to prove deadly. How does increased brain activity cause death?" Alluri inquired.

"I believe it was a combination of his advanced age and the amount of initial exposure. The aged immune system was unable to clear the excess toxins as they built up," replied Dr. Steinman.

Sasha added, "Yes, the brain and nervous system basically overheated from excessively, externally stimulated activity."

"How confident are you in your assessment? You said the bacteria was found in his blood. Is there any possibility of contamination to other employees?" asked Alluri.

"It is hard to say. We will need to conduct a thorough investigation of the clean-up crew, Mr. Grayson's family, and those that came in contact with him during his death," replied Sasha.

"The clean-up crew have already been examined, no cuts found and no bacteria in their blood. Mr. Grayson had no family, and his two cats have been eliminated and disposed appropriately, just in case. There were only two individuals that came into contact with him during his death and we are monitoring their activity until we find a suitable treatment," added Dr. Steinman.

"Monitoring? We need them in quarantine. Until we know if this spreads by any means other than direct blood contact, or if it poses a threat to anyone but the elderly, or those immune compromised. We can't take any chances," Alluri declared, shocked that the doctor had released anyone out of the confines of the lab who had been contaminated, even if it was a bacteria and not a virus.

Dr. Steinman looked dejected and responded with, "Yes sir, we will move them to quarantine immediately."

"Does the bacteria respond to standard antibiotics?" asked Alluri.

"Yes. We will need to do further testing to see how long the toxin takes to fully clear. For all we know, a normal, healthy individual maybe able to eradicate both the bacteria and toxin without antibiotics. We'll have to bring in test subjects... I estimate we will have more answers within two weeks if we start immediately," Sasha explained. Dr. Steinman nodded in agreement.

"Good. You will have all the resources you need to begin testing straightaway," responded Alluri. He liked the idea of a product that could require re-exposure, that meant increased profitability. He could see this as the next "smart pill," finally something he could sell outside of the black market.

"How has the clean-up of the Quinta virus leak been going?" Alluri asked.

"Fairly well. We still don't know how they are leaking into the lake. Every passage and run off has been checked repeatedly. I believe there must be more corridors within the old compound that we have not found," said Dr. Steinman.

"Or, more plausibly, your men are not being careful with the shipments," responded Sasha. She and Dr. Steinman just stared at each other. This was an argument Alluri had heard a dozen times, unfortunately.

"So far, we have been lucky. Every virus has not been deadly, but who knows what we will find as we continue to dig? We all need to strive to be more careful." Alluri responded as he began to think of ways to ensure no further damage could be done. *Maybe a new company safety initiative? Employees needed to feel comfortable coming forward with reports of minor injuries, like cuts, but how would he motivate them? Safety Stars program?*

"Sir, we have new data from Test Subject 17," said Dr. Steinman, interrupting Alluri's train of thought. "He is in Room 5, would you like to see? It is quite fascinating."

"Yes, of course," replied Alluri. "Lead the way."

Dr. Steinman and Sasha both left the lab and went through the cleaning room to disrobe. Alluri was steered further down into the research facility and to a large steel door. Dr. Steinman entered a code into his belt and the door opened. Inside a large room, on a small cot, sat a man wearing only light blue cotton pants. His face, chest and arms were covered in black streaks and his eyes were bloodshot, but he was smiling as he said, "Nice to see you as usual, Dr. Steinman. I see you brought company?"

"Yes, Gerry, this is Mr. Repalle and Miss Mikhailov. They have come to see what you can do," replied Dr. Steinman. "Can you please demonstrate?"

"As you wish," Gerry responded as he bowed his head slightly and walked over to a weight bench. He picked up a large barbell, with several weights, with one hand. He then flipped it into the air and caught it with the other hand. Next, he took one of the weights from the end of the barbell and broke it in half with his head, grinning like a Cheshire cat the entire time.

"Remarkable!" exclaimed Alluri. From what he could tell, the weights on that barbell added up to about

300 lbs. He walked over to pick up one of the pieces of the weight Gerry had smashed with his face, a metal coated cement. He tried to smash the piece against a large bar and the reverberations he felt back into his arm from the impact caused him to drop the piece to the ground with a loud clang. "The latest Quinta virus looks promising. Do we know how it works?"

"The virus takes over the cells in the muscle fiber, causing it to produce a concentrated carbon fiber similar to graphene in structure. The resulting muscle tissue is 100 times stronger than normal, and 10 times denser," explained Dr. Steinman. "It also can help the body withstand large electrical currents, though I am not sure Gerry would want to demonstrate that right now, would you?"

Gerry didn't not look enthusiastic. He just stood there rubbing his right arm where the skin looked red over the black streaks.

"Sasha, have you found anything dangerous about this new virus? How is the antivirus coming along?" asked Alluri.

"The muscle transformation, once initiated, is irreversible. They become a permanent carbon coating, like a tattoo on the muscle tissue. However, the anti-viral we have created, if administered early or before exposure, can limit and even prevent initiation of carbonization by the virus. In addition, the virus must be injected directly into muscle tissue in order to spread, so there is no worry about indirect contamination," replied Sasha.

"So, it is synergistic with the last 4 viruses we have found? Does Gerry here have the other four as well?"

inquired Alluri, looking over to Gerry, who was now smiling again because he wasn't going to have to demonstrate the shock proofing effects.

"Yes, Gerry is the first to have all five," Dr. Steinman said quickly, smiling and patting Gerry on the back. "If the muscle enhancement was not backed by the tendon and bone reinforcement, that little flip would have ripped his arm right off. The other two enhancements that cause increased liver enzyme and red blood cell production we believe were designed to aid in the large amount of cellular changeover needed for virus propagation. So, yes, they are extremely synergistic. Whomever developed these had a clear focus."

"Yes, a focus that we will be able to take advantage of. The Russians and the Chinese are both finding the first four in great demand. Now, with the Quinta virus, soldiers like Gerry here will be the new elite force of the world," declared Alluri. Gerry looked quite pleased with himself, and very healthy. Except for the bloodshot eyes and the fact that just below the skin there were black streaks running all along his muscles. "Are there any … negative side effects?"

"None that we have found," said Dr. Steinman. "All 20 test subjects have had improved health, strength, and even speed. It appears the firing speed of the new carbon tissue is also 200 times quicker than normal fast-twitch muscle fiber."

"It just seems too good to be true," said Sasha. "No negative side effects? I would find it hard to believe if all my testing did not confirm little chance of ill effects. It all seems positive. Even virology has come back with little chance of contamination; subcutaneous injection is the only means of dispersion in all five."

"I agree, Sasha. It does seem too good to be true. Especially with our latest findings, improved physical ability combined with mental stimulation," responded Alluri.

"Mental stimulation?" asked Gerry eagerly.

Alluri instantly regretted mentioning the latest findings from the bacteria. Gerry was obviously hooked on his enhancements, and wanted more.

"Yes, I did not realize it!" Dr. Steinmen said, enthusiastically. "Faster muscles only equals faster reaction time if the synaptic tissue is firing faster. We should start trials immediately with the bacteria and the viruses combined. This would take the entire system to the next level, with extraordinary possibilities!" exclaimed Dr. Steinman with emphatic nods from Gerry.

Sasha gave Alluri a look he had seen a thousand times, one that let him know how much of an idiot she thought Dr. Steinman was in wanting to move forward so quickly to human trials. He had been this reckless with each new virus, and seemed to be getting worse at moving forward without much testing.

"Let Sasha finish her tests with the mice, Dr. Steinman. Just because we have been lucky so far, does not mean that our luck will continue. Be patient, we will know more in two weeks," responded Alluri. Dr. Steinman looked like he was about to say something, then he cleared his throat and nodded. Sasha looked pleased.

"Now, I need to get back before my wife makes me sleep in the garage for the next week. Is there anything else I need to see?" said Alluri. "Sasha, I assume you will be staying here for the next few weeks. Do you need anything?"

"Wait, she is staying here?" asked Dr. Steinman in shock.

"Yes. Miss Mikhailov and I both believe the status quo here would benefit from having our head of research in its midst for a little while. She may also be able to solve the problem of the leaks we have been having into the lake," announced Alluri, with authority. He wanted to make sure Dr. Steinman knew he was being watched, and to be on his toes. The leaks into the lake were unacceptable, and there had been whole shipments of product disappearing lately. Something was going on, and he was sure Sasha's presence here would either root out the issue or resolve it.

Seven years ago Dr. Steinman was a regular general practitioner assigned to the mine. Now his responsibilities far outstripped his credentials. He had done a fine job in adapting, but Alluri was beginning to question his motives.

The three moved out of Gerry's room, through the steel door and into the main research floor. They walked a few feet towards where the tubes where but Dr. Steinman suddenly stopped and turned around.

"I didn't want to say this in front of Gerry, but we have had some negative side effects," said Dr. Steinman.

Both Alluri and Sasha were alarmed; this was the first they had heard of anything remotely negative about the remarkable enhancements they were finding and synthesizing for years. They both looked at each other and crossed their arms over their chests at the same time. When they realized they had both done the same thing, they both uncrossed their arms at the same time as well. Finally, Alluri cleared his throat and said, "Continue" to Dr. Steinman.

"The viruses are synergistic with each other, but they take a lot out of the body, even with the increased red blood cells and liver enzymes. Gerry is not our only test subject to take all 5 viruses, he is the only one who has survived."

"What do you mean? I thought all of the viruses caused enhancement effects," said Sasha. "All of my research has indicated positive results."

Alluri could see she was going almost as pale as she had in the helicopter as she started to mutter something he didn't understand in Russian. He felt a bit nauseated himself, *how many deaths?* When these viruses were discovered, he did everything in his power to ensure the safety of everyone working for him and in the town. He would have kept them buried or destroyed them had they had any negative effect. This news from Dr. Steinman was quite a shock, and hard to believe given the extensive testing they had performed over the last seven years.

"Yes, individually they have enhancement effects. But, when combined, especially with the last one, the Quinta virus, they take too much out on the nervous system. Some of the test subjects have already died," Dr. Steinman continued, but Sasha interrupted with,

"Why are we just now hearing about this doctor? How many have died already?"

"Two over the weekend, numbers 18 and 20, and 19 died just this morning. Please, I am not sure how much longer Gerry has to live. I believe the new bacteria is key to his survival; he may not have two weeks for your tests to complete," explained Dr. Steinman, looking directly at Sasha. She was staring him down with overt suspicion. She began to open her mouth to say something he was sure to be an insult directed at Dr. Steinman in Russian when Alluri interrupted with, "Go ahead, doctor, if it will save Gerry's life. Only Gerry though, no other human test subjects, understand?"

"Yes sir, of course. Thank you," replied Dr. Steinman. "Excuse me, I need to go make preparations for Sasha's stay here and ensure the rooms are ready for the necessary experiments. I assume you are done with me for now?"

"Yes, of course. Thank you, Dr. Steinman, I appreciate your efforts and progress," responded Alluri. He waited a minute for the doctor to enter the tubes and be out of earshot before he turned to Sasha and said, "Is there anything you need? I want to ensure your efforts here are not in vain."

"I assure you, I will be quick and thorough. As soon as I find anything, I will let you know," she responded. "I find it highly suspicious that we are just now hearing about any deaths. He did not mention a thing to me when I came down; he only focused on the old man. I find his reticence disturbing. I will route out everything he is keeping from us. Be assured, he will speak freely soon."

Sasha Mikhailov was the most competent researcher Alluri had ever met, he was sure she would do exactly what she said. She looked off in the direction the doctor had gone with a scowl, fists clinched.

"I feel like I have been down here all day. I am starting to feel claustrophobic!" Alluri declared, attempting to ease the tension.

"You own a mine and you get claustrophobia? Odd," responded Sasha looking at Alluri quizically.

"I am a mine owner, not a mine worker," replied Alluri, laughing as he made his way to the tubes. Sasha pressed a few numbers into her belt and gave him a little nod. He would have nodded back but he was already flying towards the offices above.

He was met with empty, dark silence. First shift had ended, and the only workers left were in the mine, not the offices. The center column still displayed activity in the mine, but the images were dark and there was no sound. The news stations were turned off, the lights in the offices were off and the windows showed the sun had already set. *Where did the time go?*

When he reached the heliport outside, he saw his pilot waiting. He was sitting on a bench playing a game on his expanded phone band. From what he could see through the glass, it looked like some kind of puzzle game with little stuffed animals that looked like kittens navigating a labyrinth. When he noticed Alluri standing there, the pilot replaced the band on his right arm and stood up stretching, then said, "Your wife is not going to be happy, Mr. Repalle, and I am pretty sure Zales is closed by now."

Alluri cringed, looking down at his phone band; it was already 8:15 pm. He had been married for over 25 years, and the one thing he knew for certain is that tonight he would be sleeping in the garage.

CHAPTER 7

History Lesson

Jordan always had a fascination with anything historic. Particularly wars in the great empires of ancient Rome and China. He spent the majority of his youth in libraries, nose-deep in book after book on the rise and fall of ancient civilizations. He had probably been so interested because when he was a youth he was living through the fall of one of the greatest civilizations, The United States of America. Even before the first bomb struck LA, he knew it was impending. The sudden large military spending, the loss of the gold standard, Russia's loss of key holds in the Middle East, and especially the rapid rise of India and China in technology and industry were all tell-tale signs. By the time the first bomb dropped, he had already convinced his parents to take an extended summer vacation in Wyoming.

Living through the disaster and reading about it later in history books were two different things. In real life, there was sudden panic followed by years of complete isolation from what civilization that remained. The reality was illness everywhere due to radiation dust covering all of the North American continent. Those who did not die in the initial blast either died in the following weeks or were left caring for those who were dying even more slowly, such as Jordan's parents. They died two years after the dust reached Wyoming. There was no help, but there were also no invaders to fight because the whole world had fallen apart. It was just death, loss and loneliness. It would be years before communities came together again with the help of the International Alliance to re-establish what remained of the people of the United States and Canada.

According to history, when the President of the USA retaliated against North Korea for the first bomb that made it into USA by basically obliterating all of North Korea, everyone else who had a nuclear bomb decided to use theirs at once. Russian decided to launch an attack on all major US cities simultaneously, as well as major targets in Europe. Anti-ballistic missiles were able to stop most of the bombs, but the few that got through were enough to cause total worldwide chaos. China took advantage of the disaster, with their own interests being control of all of Asia. However, they were stopped in their pursuit by India and Russia. India with the help of USA military overseas and British allies that remained in Europe had taken out Pakistan. Their coalition had conquered through most of the Middle East into Saudi Arabia by the time they stopped. After three and half years of bloody warfare, India and their allies were caught by Russia, who controlled the vast majority of Europe to the North, and China, who controlled almost all of Asia on the east.

The continental USA was left in nuclear dust, isolated and alone, no longer even seen as a threat with China, India and Russia emerging as the global leaders. International laws were set in place to completely remove all nuclear technology and put limits to military spending by any one country. The large increase in military spending that the President of the USA had pushed for in the USA was seen as a direct threat to Russia, and was their excuse for the attack.

What was left of the United States and Canada pulled itself together on Christian values, hard work and community which they believed was the pillar of what had made the nation great.

The war was also blamed on the greed and selfishness of capitalism, and due to the help of China in re-establishing the economy and law, current communities were heavily influenced by communist order.

That was history. But, the reality was that nothing seemed all that different now than what Jordan could remember from his youth before the bombs and dust. He still spent the vast majority of his time in libraries and researching on the Internet. People still went to work, the grocery store, and home every night. Technology was still advancing at a rapid pace, selling to the highest bidder, capitalism or no capitalism. Everyone and their brother was taking advantage of the vast land and mineral resource of the Americas that had previously been protected, similar to right before the war. Plus, the superpowers of India, China and Russia were in a cold war standoff that could blow up any second. To Jordan, it felt just like living in the USA before the war.

His interest in the rise and fall of civilizations was still strong, even after living through a fall. Today he was researching the Indian tribes that lived here before

Europeans settled the area. He had started looking up Navajo details to prove to Catherine they weren't a tunneling people and had come across some interesting information about viruses as well that might help him answer what was going on at the mine.

He was particularly interested in signs of viruses that wiped everyone out. He did not expect to come across an article from the 1860s about an illness that wiped out the entire settlement that was known as Mesa Heights. The illness was blamed on a nearby Native American population, which was quickly dispatched by state militia.

He had never heard of Mesa Heights. Supposedly, it was a mostly Dutch population that had migrated west for gold mining. He did a little more research and found that this entire desert region was once called Mesa Heights. Despite its past, it had become a thriving mining community again until the 1950 when it was wiped out by another strange illness. After this last incident, the entire town was abandoned.

The name of the town, Desert Grande, wasn't introduced until 15 years ago with the arrival of Greggo Sands. Until then, there was practically no population.

Jordan never knew any of this, mostly because his past searching was on the history of Desert Grande. Now he had a treasure trove of information, and it was both thrilling and frightening, by searching for hits on Mesa Heights. What was the mysterious illness that kept wiping out the population in the area? Were there any survivors who could tell the tale from the 1950's? Most of the people here were assigned within the last

10 years, himself include, when Greggo Sands decided to make it a model town for their new ceramic roads.

Jordan performed a search of Census data from the 1950s, finding no population. Though no one remained from the 1950s, anyone who lived there pre-war might know more about the area and its history. He then searched 1960s, then 1970s with nothing. However, he found a few families that moved here in the 1980s. It was probably considered a retirement community by then because almost everyone was over 60 and very few families had children.

He finally found one with children who might be alive today. The Jahren family consisted of four people, two were kids. According to the 1980 Census, both Martin and Beth Jahren's occupation was listed as research scientist. They had two young sons: Clifford and Daniel, age four and seven, respectively. Census data indicated that this family remained in the area at least until the 2010 Census. He wrote down the address listed on file and the names listed for the two boys.

Jordan then performed a search for any news articles on Daniel Jahren, finding a news article that stated both him and his brother had opened up a research department and were hiring in 2007 in southern Colorado. Another article written in 2010, as a homegrown pride feature, had a picture of the two brothers. The men were dressed as doctors, accepting an award for advancements in prosthetics at an international medical convention. The last article in 2017, unfortunately, was an obituary. It listed both Daniel and Clifford as being assumed deceased following an explosion at their research facility. The explosion had killed everyone inside. No more new articles followed and the newspaper went out of print less than a year later. The research facility must have been the primary business in the town of Mesa Heights, because everyone left town and there was no one left according to the 2020 Census, the last census taken before the war began.

The research into the two Jahren brothers had reached a dead end, literally. Jordan was disappointed. He had hoped to use the address on file and track one of the brothers down to discuss the history of Mesa Heights. He wanted to know about the mysterious illness that wiped out the population in the 1860s and 1950s. Now he had even more questions and no answers.

Jordan sat back from the computer at the library and began to rub his temples. He stared at the picture of the two brothers for a while; they looked so proud and happy it made him sick. Suddenly, he realized he saw something odd about the younger brother, Clifford. There was a small amount of what looked like black streaks coming down the side of Clifford Jahren's hand as he held up the prosthetic arm for the picture. The streaking pattern looked exactly like the description of the latest virus discovered at Lake Holt, the Quinta virus.

That made Jordan think of something Catherine had said in the woods. *Didn't she say that she had dreamed of a "cyborg" who had said something about a brother, and a lab?* These were brothers, who worked on prosthetics and ran a lab in the local area. This seemed like too much of a coincidence. Jordan printed out the news article with the picture of the two brothers to show Catherine.

What exactly did Catherine say? He had been behind her while she was talking, ignoring most of what she was saying, taking in the ample view. She had a gentle sway to her hips as she walked that he found mesmerizing. She had said something about a cyborg man being asleep in her dream. That had been a bit strange. Dreaming of a dreaming person.

He would have to ask her more at school. It would give him a reason to talk to her, which he found pleasant. Not that he expected anything to come from it; he was twice her age and had been alone most of his adult life. He had no idea how to incorporate someone into his life right now, and hated change. But, he enjoyed making her smile, and her nattering wasn't all that unpleasant compared to most. He especially liked the way she looked with her hair down, in a mess, with a few leaves stuck in it ... with her breathing heavy ... his mind began to wander, then he remembered he was in a public library and pulled his thoughts out of the gutter and packed up to go home. His research on the viruses could wait until tomorrow.

Monday couldn't come soon enough. The article Jordan was keeping in his left pocket felt like it was made of burning coal. All he wanted to do was hand it to Catherine and see what her reaction would be – impressed he hoped. His students were extra irritating today. Year after year they were getting dumber and this year's class was, by far, the dumbest. Not one could name the first president of the United States, much less the last. If the information wasn't right in front of them, or the event wasn't happening right now, they didn't care.

"One merit for whoever can answer the next question," Jordan announced, hoping that would get their attention. A few students seemed to perk up at the offer. This merit system had its flaws, and he never had too much success getting involvement. *How did Elisabeth do it?*

"Name one of the Indian tribes that once lived here in Colorado." Jordan's offer was met with blank stares all around. "Just one, take a guess, anyone?" Jordan continued. *Not a single student could name a single tribe, not a single one!?!* Jordan was pacing up and down the aisle between students and trying not to lose his temper.

"I got one, Mr. Muntz," chimed in a tall, lanky, dust-blond-haired stoner in the back of the class named Edward Paulson.

"Go ahead, Mr. Paulson," Jordan replied, hoping for an answer that wouldn't make him want to throw his digiTeacher Controller against the wall.

"The Shoeshiners," Edwards said, meekly.

"Shoeshiners? You mean Shoshone?" Jordan responded.

"Yeah, man, the Shoeshiners, they all got wiped out by Big Foot," Edward said, barely containing his laughter.

"Thank you, Mr. Paulson, but there were no 'Shoeshiners' in Colorado," Jordan declared, irritated enough for the large vein in his forehead to start to pulse. He rubbed his temples with his left hand while his right hand shook slightly from the restraint of holding onto his controller.

"Of course not anymore, they got wiped out by ..." Edward began.

Jordan interrupted with, "There was never any 'Big Foot' either, Mr. Paulson. There was, however, a Native American tribe called the Shoshone, of whom Sacagawea belonged. Does anyone remember her significance in American history?"

"She helped Lewis and Clark scout the West," answered Angela Freeman, a bone-thin, bleach-blond sophomore with big blue eyes and fake dark eyebrows.

"Thank you, Miss Freeman, that is correct. You just earned yourself a merit," Jordan replied. "Sacagawea worked as a translator, and proved invaluable at ensuring the Lewis and Clark exposition's safe passage through territory that was predominately controlled by the Shoshone at the time."

The bell rang and everyone began to quickly leave and Jordan announced, "Tomorrow, we will discuss more about the Native Americans of this area. Please do your research in order to be prepared for questions in class."

Angela presented her digiStudent to get her merit and quickly left the classroom. Edward came up right behind her and asked if he could get a merit too, for his participation.

"Mr. Paulson, you are lucky that you are not at Principal Repalle's office right now, you understand?" Edward looked confused, but Jordan just gave him a blank stare until he gave up and walked away.

Jordan sat down at his desk and felt a bit troubled. He pulled out the paper in his pocket that he planned to show Catherine. Did she care about history? What was he doing, trying to impress her with knowledge? He thought about throwing the paper away, about skipping lunch.

His next class was senior level world history. He knew these students well. Most had classes with him for the last 3.5 years, so they knew him well too. Not one student was smiling once they walked into the room and saw his demeanor. No one liked pop quiz day, and when he was in a bad mood, it was always pop quiz day. As he put a current map of the world on the front wall, he heard groaning all throughout the classroom. He smiled; their misery made him feel just a little better.

"Pop quiz. Please use the map shown to mark the controlled territories of the major superpowers of the world. Then, mark each of the major countries described in class last week that no longer exist since WWIII," Jordan Muntz declared as he sat back in his chair to take in the wonderful, terrified looks on the students' faces.

The bell rang and the class did not move, they were all still staring at the wall in horror and busy typing into their digiStudents. Muntz turned off the front wall and stated, "Please submit your final answers now, or none of your work will be counted." He thought he heard a few cuss words from the back of the class; that almost brought a smile to his face.

There were a few stragglers, so he decided to count down aloud "5, 4, 3, 2 ..." and by then all had submitted their answers. "Thank you, I look forward to grading these this afternoon."

"It looks like your whole class is going to a funeral, Jordan. What did you do to them?" Elisabeth asked, standing right outside the doorway.

"Pop quiz," replied one of the students morosely, as he brushed by her on his way out of the door.

"Yes, I just thought I would check to see if the class remembered anything I said last week," Jordan responded. "From what I can see, they did not."

"A quiz on a Monday? You are particularly evil, Jordan, especially considering most of these students did have to go to a funeral this weekend," said Elisabeth as she headed out to the faculty lounge, shaking her head and patting one of the forlorn kids reassuringly on the back.

Jordan followed, a few steps behind. He watched as she engaged some of the students with little waves of her hand, and smiles, even a "hello, blah blah blah." *How was she always so cheery? Why did the students like her so much?* He was exhausted just being witness to it all. Maybe Catherine was right, maybe Elisabeth was on drugs. That thought made him smile. *Sign me up for the happy drugs!* he thought as he pictured himself walking through the halls, high fiving the students, skipping even.

Jordan was in line behind Elisabeth at the combinator in the faculty lounge. She turned around to see the little smirk on his lips and then acted like she was going to pass out as she exclaimed, "Oh my god, Muntz is smiling, everyone!"

"I don't believe it," Jordan heard behind him, then turned to see that it was Catherine, smiling herself, dimples and all, looking up at him with those doe-brown eyes. She had her hair down today in little waves around her face that made her look even more sweet and innocent than usual.

"He must have had a good weekend marking student papers with F's I presume," stated Elisabeth. "Your schadenfreude finally giving you a high, Jordan?"

"No, just wondering what kind of drugs you're on, Elisabeth," he responded nonchalantly, no longer smiling and face back to the controlled expression he worked so hard on perfecting all these years.

"Oh, the best kind of drugs. Sunshine, clean air and exercise. I spent the weekend backpacking in the San Juan National Forest with a group of friends and my vitamin D levels are peaking. You should try getting outdoors sometime," Elisabeth said. "You might stop looking like Skeletor's cousin 'Bob the snob.'"

"I don't think the wilderness works that way with him, Elisabeth," Catherine replied. "He looked just as grouchy as ever when I came across him hiking Saturday."

"Now that is a story, you two went hiking together? What did handsome Anthony have to say about that?" Elisabeth asked as she pulled her Tikka Masala out of the combinator. She stayed at the line, bringing the bowl up to smell her food, savoring it almost as much as she was savoring the looks on both Catherine's and Jordan's faces as she eyed them both up, down and sideways. "Wow, you both look like you were caught doing something naughty."

Jordan looked over to see Catherine blushing. It was then that he recalled the conversation about "camping," and the kiss he placed on her hand as he left her in the parking lot of the trailhead. He felt protective of her, and wanted to defend her.

"We ran into each other. She was out walking her boyfriend's dog. Don't you have anything better to do than to start rumors and gossip Elisabeth?"

"I thought you said you were going to the funeral this weekend, Elisabeth," said Catherine. "Did you skip the funeral to go camping?"

"I did go to the funeral. I support my students in their time of need, unlike you two. It was Sunday afternoon; I got back Sunday morning. It was very sad to see the Armstrong children dealing with the loss of their father. They read a poem together and barely made it through. It seems the whole family is going to be relocated to Oklahoma, so that is good news," responded Elisabeth. "I have family in Oklahoma, a cousin, I wouldn't mind being re-assigned there myself."

Jordan retrieved his Tikka Masala from the combinator and couldn't decide what to do. He wanted to sit with Catherine so he could show her the paper, but if he sat down now she might not follow him to his table. He decided to take a little extra time getting utensils and napkins, then casually stood next to Elisabeth.

"How many children did Larry Armstrong have, Elisabeth?" he asked.

"Three. They were 17-, 10- and 4-years-old. Josh was the only one we all knew, the other two were too young. His wife is a homemaker, so she is getting relocated to be near family to help raise the children. She didn't seem that sad. I speculate that Larry might have been abusive," Elisabeth replied.

"There you are spreading rumors again, Elisabeth. What proof do you have?" Jordan questioned. She always seemed to be in everyone's business.

Elisabeth responded quickly with, "Experience, wisdom and age, my young friend. When my husband died, I was a mess. I could barely hold it together. She was almost cheerful. The only time that I saw her cry was when her children read that poem, though I don't think a single person in the room didn't cry."

"What makes you think he was abusive, Elisabeth? That seems like a far-fetched claim," Catherine inquired as she got her lunch and headed towards the nearest empty table. Elisabeth and Jordan both followed, taking the vacant seats on either side of Catherine.

"Just a hunch," she said, noticing that Jordan had followed them to the table. "Speaking of hunches, what exactly went on during this 'accidental' hike together this weekend? How did you get that cut on your cheek, Catherine? Are you being abused? Jordan, did you abuse her?" Elisabeth remarked slyly. She then began digging into her curried chicken and rice, scooping it up with pieces of naan bread. She would suck the masala off of the bread before eating the bread, which Jordan found repulsive and irksome.

"Nothing, really. Anthony's dog, Rufus, nearly ripped my arm off chasing a squirrel up a tree. He threw me right into a large pile of sticks and mud, that's how I got the cut on my cheek," Catherine responded. "No one is abusing me. Please don't spread those rumors, Elisabeth!"

"So, Jordan threw you into a pile of sticks and mud and he is not abusing you?" asked Elisabeth between bites.

"No, the dog, Rufus, threw her," replied Jordan. "That dog is a beast, he could have killed her."

"He is a lot to handle, but I love that furry monster," Catherine stated, beaming. Before Elisabeth could say anything snarky, Catherine added, "I love the dog, not Jordan, and no one is abusing me, okay?" She started picking at her food; she had gotten the palak paneer, a creamed spinach, and looked like she was regretting it.

"Where was Anthony?" asked Elisabeth. "Oh wait, he had that hunting trip, didn't he? Convenient. When the cats away, the mouse will play."

"What are you implying?" demanded Catherine.

"She's just messing with you again, Catherine. She knows damn well nothing would ever happen between the two of us; she just likes to rile you up," said Jordan, still somewhat jilted by the "I don't love Jordan" remark Catherine just made.

"You are particularly entertaining, my young friend," replied Elisabeth, laughing. "Oh, to be young and innocent again!"

Jordan was picking at his meal as well. Not because he didn't like the food, tikka masala was one of his favorite dishes, but because he was trying to work up to pulling out the folded paper in his pocket to show Catherine. He finally just reached into his pocket and slid it over in front of her.

Jordan looked intently to see Catherine's reaction. She delicately unfolded the paper, then gasped aloud clenching her chest. She began mouthing the words in the article aloud as she read.

"Passing notes, are we?" inquired Elisabeth as she leaned over to see. "Next, you will be playing footsie under the table."

"It's none of your business, Elisabeth," Jordan responded, pushing her hand back as she tried to reach for the paper. He then took a big bite of his naan and sat back in contentment. He was enjoying gloating over Elisabeth's scowl and Catherine's attention on the object he brought. Catherine obviously was fascinated.

"Where did you find this, Jordan?" Catherine demanded and then she whispered, "How is this possible?"

"I was doing a bit of research in the library, searching old news articles in microfiche, and I came across this one. I thought you might be interested based on what you told me the other day. I plan to do more research tomorrow; you are welcome to join me," he responded, but quickly regretted the invitation. Catherine had looked up quickly, blushed, and looked down even more quickly. She was looking a little too intently at the paper now, as if trying to not to look at him.

"Sounds like a date to me," said Elisabeth, smirking.

She sure knows how to make an awkward situation worse! Jordan thought.

"I can't. I have to prepare midterms, and then I have to grade them. It will be a busy week for me, I'm sorry," Catherine replied, hesitantly. She seemed to be picking her words carefully, so not to hurt his feelings. "I'm already behind grading the last-minute assignment I gave my Medieval Literature class Friday afternoon."

"I understand," Jordan replied, quickly finishing his meal. As he was getting ready to leave, Catherine grabbed his hand and looked up at him and said simply, "Thank you."

"I'll let you know tomorrow what I find during my research tonight," he replied. He was feeling mixed emotions, mostly thrilled. Her hands were so soft and delicate. He looked over to see Elisabeth shaking her head at him, again. He gave her as blank a stare as he could and hurried away.

CHAPTER 8

Dacdream a Little Dream of Me

Catherine spent her evening grading the two-page essays she had assigned her class on the video of *Canterbury Tales*. Unfortunately, some of the kids had decided to follow her example and take a long nap during the video. She had just marked up the fourth student who thought the tales were about something silly like chocolate rabbits that lived in medieval times in a town called Canterbury England, where they now make all kinds of chocolates. *There is no way they could have gotten that from watching the video!* She put her digiTeacher Controller down long enough to rub her temples and take a few deep breaths. It was partially her fault, she did sleep through the whole class and set a bad example. *Maybe if she let them all slide on this assignment no one would rat her out to the principal? Why did she give them this assignment in the first place?* That's right, she had thought telling them they would have an essay on the video would make them pay attention and not look back and notice her sleeping. She was obviously wrong.

Sass picked up her head from Catherine's lap and then jumped up to plant a few licks on her cheek. "Thank you for the kisses, sweet lady," Catherine said as she scratched behind Sass's fluffy ears. She looked over at her phone band to check the time. The rest of the grading would have to wait for tomorrow; it was already past 10 p.m. "It's time for bed, isn't it?" Sass gave a little, 'woof' in confirmation.

Catherine made her way to the bedroom with Sass at her feet. She was too tired to even shower tonight; she would just have to wake up a little earlier to take one in the morning. She threw on a nightgown and plunged right into her sheets. She set the alarm to display the milky-way galaxy spinning above her. It was always so soothing to watch and it was guaranteed to put her to sleep right away. Staring up at the ceiling, her mind started to move through the events of the day, processing what was important for retention and everything else to forget-me-land.

Her mind stopped at lunch, with the smug look on Jordan's face as he handed her a folded piece of paper. The visual impression of what was inside that piece of paper would be forever burned on the back of her eyeballs. Two brothers, heralded by the local press and accepting an award for advances in prosthetics research. The face of the eldest brother stood out like it was painted in gold fairy dust in her mind's eye. Her body even remembered her reaction to seeing the article, and was replaying it for her as she thought about it again. For a second, her heart had stopped and she had forgotten to breath. She was staring at the man who had been in her dreams. A person she had never met in her entire life and thought was a figment of her imagination. *It was beyond coincidence, wasn't it? What did it all mean?* She had done such a good job of putting him out of her head all day, but now it was all she could think about.

She felt a shaky chill all throughout her body that ran deep into her bones and she pulled her sheets and comforter closer. *What did this all mean?* That thought kept repeating, over and over. *Maybe the mysterious cyborg man from the news article would be in her dreams tonight and she could ask him more questions? Maybe he would actually answer this time, now that she knew who he was and she confronted him with his identity?* She almost laughed at the idea of confronting a figment of her imagination. *Why not?*

She needed to relax her mind to fall asleep, which meant she needed to stop thinking about the news article and clear her head. She let her mind keep processing the rest of the day as usual and took deep breaths to relax. The rest of the day moved by in a flash and faded. The images ended with her imagination producing giant chocolate rabbits getting their heads cut off by her digiTeacher stylus and the chocolate heads landing on the desks of students in her classroom that hadn't been paying attention.

As her thoughts and reactive images faded, she began to fly straight into the stars from the projection above her bed. In her dreams the Milky Way was made of milk. As her hand glided over to grab a twinkling blue star the milk dispersed all around her. The white milk became fluffy clouds encompassing her. The clouds then dissipated into a finer and finer mist. As the mist cleared, the surrounding scene became a red cliff overlooking the city of Desert Grande. It was a cliff she had hiked by several times since she had been assigned to the city, but she had never gone up to the top. She had wanted to go to the top, and had looked up and wondered what it was like many times but there was no trail to the top that she could find.

Her bare toes were on the smooth surface of petrified sand dunes that made up the top of the cliff. It was noon on a sunny summer day and the rock sparkled like a million little stars. There were little pools of clear water in the recesses of the cliff face, with dragonflies skipping across the water. The dragonflies glowed in all colors of the rainbow. The air smelled like the jasper trees and sage bushes of the surrounding woods. She opened her arms to feel the warm summer breeze blow through her silk nightgown, sending her robe flying back behind her like a cape. She felt like the wind moved around her body and hugged her like the greeting of a long lost friend.

"You look like a goddess," she heard behind her, in an all too familiar voice. She turned around to see the golden eyes of the mechanical man she expected. The normal flickering of his eyes where replaced by bright reflections from the sun. It was unsettling and almost looked like they were flashlights. The bright noon sun was suddenly a sunset, with muffled rosy tones. The flashing eyes were no longer blindingly bright, but subdued like the sunset.

"You have such control. Such vivid dreams. I find it irresistible to watch you," he said with a smile that did not reach his eyes as he walked over to within a foot of Catherine. There was a metal click and the sound of moving gears with every movement of his body as he moved closer.

Catherine could see the familiar, but completely foreign, symbols move across his eyes clearly from this distance and was trying to make them out. The symbols looked like something from an Aztec ruins, possibly the Nahuatl language, but with numbers mixed in and possibly Latin.

"Do you know why I am here?" he asked, breaking her stare.

"Yes, you want me to 'close the mine.' Hey, if I have such control over my dreams, then why would I dream of you telling me to do something so ludicrous?" retorted Catherine.

The mechanical man began to laugh hysterically. "Ludicrous?" he laughed more, the sound becoming more and more maniacal. "You have NO IDEA of the dangers that will be unleashed if they continue!"

"Then tell me all about it, Dr. Daniel Jahren," Catherine replied haughtily. The news article that Jordan had given her earlier was unmistakable; this man was the older brother of the two doctors, the one named Daniel Jahren. Of course, in the article he had hair instead of a half-bald head and half-metal plate with small objects sticking out the side that looked like they could be antenna.

He looked at Catherine with as blank an expression as she had ever seen, except there was something very cold about his eyes that sent shivers down her spine. She pulled her robe around her instinctively, even though it was a sunny, warm day. She had no idea what he was thinking.

"You are remarkable," he finally said, but with still no expression on his face. It was almost as if he was purposefully trying not to betray his feelings.

"So, you are Daniel? How are you in my dreams? What is so dangerous about the mines? How can I stop the mining? Why should I be the one to stop the mining? What is truly going on here?" Catherine demanded, pouring out the questions like canon fire. The barrage took Daniel back a step or two, literally. He walked back with every question. Then, he looked like he might walk away or disappear in his normal flash. But, after a terribly indecisive minute that made Catherine hold her breath, he finally decided to stay.

"Your dreams call to me, you wouldn't understand how I ...." he began but seemed to be troubled. "I just want to sleep. I need to sleep, Catherine. The digging is going to wake me up."

"And that is dangerous? How?" she asked.

"You know my name, which means you should know something about the viruses that have been part of the history of this area, correct?" Daniel inquired looking at Catherine, who was looking very confused at the moment. "Ah, I can see that you don't know about the viruses. History is a funny thing ... easily erased, easily changed, easily buried. You need to ask about the viruses, then you will understand. There's more ..." he looked at her, seeming to weigh his words and continued, "but that should be enough for anyone to stop digging in that godforsaken tomb of a mine."

"Viruses? Like the ones at the lake caused by the mosquitoes?" asked Catherine, perplexed. Those were the only viruses she knew about, and none of them were deadly or dangerous as far as she knew. "Jordan did say that he thought the mine had something to do with the viruses at the lake."

"Jordan? Who is Jordan?" Daniel seemed very curious, stepping forward again towards Catherine.

"He is just a co-worker, a History teacher actually: Jordan Muntz. He was the one who found the article about you and your brother working on prosthetics research and development that had your name," Catherine replied. *Why did he care who Jordan was?*

Daniel walked to within a few inches of Catherine, looking down on her ominously. He then closed his eyes. He began to flicker in and out of Catherine's dream. He disappeared fully for a minute, but without his typical flash of light that tended to wake Catherine up.

"This Jordan has very jumbled dreams, but he clearly has a thing for you," Daniel said as he re-appeared.

Catherine was blushing. She knew Jordan liked her. If the kiss on the hand after the hike wasn't enough, when he asked her over today to do "research" with him it sounded a lot like a date request. "What is wrong with someone liking me?" she asked, abashed.

"I see," he stated, looking down on her intently. He then disappeared again for another couple of minutes and when he came back he was frowning and said, "I would watch out for this guy. He is not what he seems and his intentions towards you are ... troubling." He looked like he highly disapproved of Jordan.

"Why should you care about his intentions towards me?"

"You are ...." Daniel paused, then continued with, "special to me."

"So, I am supposed to not have a relationship with a man because a guy in my dreams who says that he 'needs to sleep' thinks I am special to him?" Catherine replied, completely confused. She didn't know if she was flattered or angry.

"No, he is not what you think. His dreams are ..." he looked as if he was trying to think of what to say then continued with "disturbing. They indicate an unstable mind."

"Well, he seems to be the only one who knows anything about what is going on around here. And you don't seem to want to tell me anything. Who should I trust?" answered Catherine.

"I am sorry, you are right. I don't think you understand how special you are, how special all of this ..." he stopped himself. He then walked over to the edge of the cliff, near one of the little ponds and opened his arms, looking around at the rose-colored sunset scene, on a cliff overlooking the city. A purple glowing dragonfly landed on his finger, and he laughed as he continued, "Not everyone can dream like this, Catherine."

"Is that why you visit me?" responded Catherine. "To play with my dragonflies and watch the sunset?"

"Yes, and no," Daniel replied, slowly. "I do enjoy your dreams, and miss them when I can't find you. Why did you not sleep the other night? There were two nights where you were gone this week."

Catherine was swiftly disturbed at the thought of this man watching her *every night* and wasn't sure if she wanted to say anything. She was having trouble wrapping her head around how any of this could even be real; she was in a dream right now talking to a cyborg, after all. She finally answered, "My boyfriend, Anthony, he kept me up snoring all night one night."

"Boyfriend? I would never have thought you had a boyfriend. Why is he never in your dreams? Is this a new relationship? Most people dream of their significant other on a regular basis," Daniel inquired, quite shocked, stepping even closer with each question, and seemingly looming by the end. He was looming over her a lot tonight. He had never been this close before and this was the third time he had come so close in one night.

Catherine didn't want to answer; she didn't know how to answer. He had a point. Her dreams were filled with the things that made her happy, and Anthony was never in them. That probably wasn't a good sign for their relationship.

"What is his name?" Daniel said in a tone that made it sound like an order.

Catherine knew he was likely going to do that flicker and eavesdrop thing he had just done when she mentioned Jordan, but she was curious what he would find: "His name is Anthony Grant."

Of course, she was right. Immediately, Daniel flicked in and out, then he was gone. Catherine waited, he was gone for a while before he appeared again. She had been sitting cross-legged on the edge of the cliff, playing with her dragonflies. She was getting them to create a glowing rainbow around her when he materialized beside her and made them scatter in every direction.

"Anthony is sick. You must stay away from him," Daniel said, this time it was definitely an order.

"Sick? Like what kind of sick?" Catherine demanded as she stood up to face Daniel. She was very confused. Last time she saw Anthony he was as healthy as an ox. *Did he mean he had a mental illness? Like was he dreaming of sheep or something?*

"He was exposed to one of the tests we were running at the lab. We could never control this specific strain we had developed very well; it was unpredictable. So, we ended the experiment fairly early after a few test subjects died. Most tolerated the side effects of the neurotoxin well, but some had what we called a 'runaway reaction.' We were able to save a few of the runaways if we caught it in time. Once they started to convulse and emit blood from their ears and eyes, the only thing that could stop the overheating in their cerebral cortex was ice administered directly to the carotid arteries followed by intravenous penicillin," Daniel explained. He looked at Catherine and in a grave tone stated, "Don't kiss him, the contaminant is spread via bodily liquids, like saliva. Especially don't …"

Catherine knew where he was going and interrupted with, "Don't kiss him, right? That's convenient. Don't kiss my boyfriend. For how long? Shouldn't I just get him some penicillin?"

He looked at her for a minute, seemingly weighing his options. "Sure, get him some penicillin," he said, "If you can get it to him in time."

Catherine didn't know what to think, but something made her believe she should be very worried about Anthony right now.

"He brought you into the mine? What did you find?"

How did he know that? Catherine thought, he must have seen something in Anthony's dream, or hers, though she didn't remember dreaming about going into the mine. "Nothing much, just some rectangular holes and broken glass. I wanted to see if you were real, if the lab you mentioned was real. I still find it hard to believe in your ... existence," Catherine responded as she struggled internally to figure out just what she believed.

Daniel walked forward and looked Catherine directly in the eye and said, "I am real. And you are in real danger if you don't get that mining stopped now."

Chills ran down her spine. His eyes were mystifying this close and his presence emitted a pulse in the air that could be felt and heard in low vibrating tones. In fact, looking this close to him she could see ripples warping her dream coming off his body. She answered him with, "Why? Just because you will wake up? What is so dangerous about that?"

"I told you, look into the viruses. You wouldn't understand the rest, and I would have to show you ... it's just too dangerous," replied Daniel. He looked down on her, his face was inches from her face now. He was almost a foot taller but was leaning down and then he reached his hand towards her hair. From this vantage point she could gauge his expression a little better and the look in his eyes verged on pain. "Just, close the mine, okay? Goodnight," he said as he closed his eyes.

"Wait, how?" Catherine asked, in vain. Daniel had already disappeared in a blazing light. *How did he do that? Actually, how did he appear in her dreams at all? This was all just so bizarre!*

The fact that he watched her every night was creepy. But his existence proved the ability to appear in and look at other people's dreams. The thought of anyone being able to look into another person's dream was exciting. *How did he do that? He said she had extreme control in her dreams, maybe she could too?* Anthony might die and she wanted to see him and warn him. She closed her eyes and concentrated on Anthony.

Images of Anthony flashed in front of her and then settled on him lying in a hammock, holding up a turkey leg like a microphone, singing in between bites of turkey. It was never-ending turkey, because after each bite the turkey leg would reform. He sounded like Frank Sinatra, singing 'The Way You Look Tonight.' The whole screen was a bit blurry and besides the hammock, turkey leg and singing Anthony in Hawaiian hula-dancing-girl boxer shorts ... there was nothing. Just white fogginess everywhere else. Everything and everyone, including the hammock were just suspended in nothingness.

"Anthony?" Catherine almost whispered. She couldn't believe it! *Was she imagining this or was she in his dream?* It didn't seem like her typical dream; it was all so unclear, unsubstantial.

"Catherine?" Anthony said in shock. He went to get up out of his hammock and instead flipped upside down, turkey leg flying into the air. The spinning hammock suddenly stopped and he was standing where the hammock used to be. His clothes had changed as well; he was now wearing what he wore on their date last week. He leaned down to kiss her and the whole world changed; they were now lying down in her bed. The bed was only half formed and the entirety of her room was dusky mist.

"Wait, I have to tell you something," Catherine said, shocked that he was so forward in her dream: he was trying to undress her! "You're sick, you need penicillin." He continued to kiss her, she wasn't sure he understood. "Anthony, Babe, listen, you're sick."

He wasn't listening. She couldn't change the scene to make him move away or listen. She normally could change anything in her dreams and the inability to change made her feel panicked and almost claustrophobic in the all-encompassing darkness in the room. *Maybe she was actually in his dream and that is why nothing was changing?* She closed her eyes and imagined the cliff from earlier. She was back, but Anthony was gone.

She closed her eyes again and thought of Anthony. She opened her eyes again and was standing in her bedroom at the edge of a not-fully-formed bed, watching him make out with what appeared to be her. Except the other her was dressed in somewhat the same nightgown but not quite. The version of her making out with Anthony looked different too: her hair was up like she wears it to school and her hands were all over him pulling off his clothes, which she hadn't been doing. Then, the other her began to undress herself. Catherine had to look away, because it all felt positively weird and uncomfortable to watch.

Catherine closed her eyes and when she opened them again she was back on the cliff overlooking the city below.

Could she have really just visited Anthony's dream? He was normally not that sexual. Maybe it was just her projection of him? She could text him in the morning to see if he had any weird dreams. If he didn't remember his dream or if she didn't truly visit his dream then she would have to tell him about the penicillin he needed in person. If she told him about the penicillin she would have to tell him how she knew he needed the penicillin. That would be a fun conversation that she didn't even know how to begin.

She sat on the cliff, looking out at a purple sunset fading into city lights for miles all around. She usually just let her dreams take her wherever, enjoying the view. But, now she was wondering about all the lights across the valley. *Did they mean something? Were there people down below?*

She decided that she would focus on one of the lights below. It became stronger and came into focus. A street light in front of a house flickered into a small boy sleeping in blue pajamas on a red racecar bed. The next thing she knew, she was standing on a toy race track with toy cars flying all around her, bouncing off the track. Above her was the little boy. He was now a giant holding the flying cars that she had seen bouncing above and beside her on the track. He looked down at her and put down one of the cars so that he could reach for her. As his giant fingers came close to gripping her she closed her eyes and concentrated on the cliff she had been standing on earlier. When she re-opened her eyes, she was back on the cliffside.

Her heart was beating fast. She waited on the cliff for her heart to calm down and her breathing to get back to normal, staring down at the lights. *Where they all people? Who were they?* The lights flickered, some going out completely, some coming on for the first time. As she looked down at the lights, she felt connected. There was a hum in the air that vibrated in her bones and pulsed with the lights. As she focused on the pulse, she felt like all the lights at once were drawing her in and the pulse was getting stronger within her. She pushed away the pulse and all the lights went out at once. The valley below was dark. Slowly, the lights came back on, one by one. *What had she done? Did she just wake up everyone in the whole town?*

Was this all just her imagination? Daniel, the cyborg, had turned out to not be just her imagination. The picture Jordan showed her today proved he was real. *But what did that mean?* All along she had felt that his appearances were different, deep down. That is why she wanted to go into a dark, dangerous mine in the middle of the night when Anthony presented an opportunity. The fact that she found what looked like a lab, after Daniel had mentioned it in her dream, almost made her believe in and of itself. She just didn't want to believe yet. But she had to believe once she saw the evidence literally staring her back in the face from the news article.

The more she thought about Daniel spying on her, the more it gave her chills. Those golden flashes of strange symbols in his eyes was haunting. They made her feel so exposed, almost naked. She suddenly looked all around her on the cliff to see if he was watching her again. She was alone, and thankfully clothed in her silk nightgown and robe.

The cliff began to feel softer and softer beneath her. As she sunk into its embrace there was a sunrise forming over the valley below, glowing in soft yellow and orange as the sky above her was turning blue. There was an alarm ringing in the distance, getting closer and closer and it was drawing her away. She wondered how much of this she would even remember when she awoke.

CHAPTER 9

A Little Pep in Your Step

Catherine opened her eyes and sat straight up. She reached for her phone band and swiftly texted Anthony, asking him to meet her for lunch. She was surprised to see another text message from a strange number. All the message said was, "We need to talk." She texted back, "Who is this?" and stared at the screen in bewilderment. She waited a couple of minutes. No response. She needed to get in the shower now, or she would be late, again. She put down the band and got ready for work.

In the car ride over, she kept looking for a reply from either Anthony or the strange number. It was driving her crazy and she was so distracted looking down at her arm that her driving was crazy. She eventually had to put her vehicle on autopilot going down her favorite hill because she hugged a couple of the turns a little too tightly, knocking a few rocks down the steep hillside into the trees below. She never noticed how far of a drop it was from that hillside until she almost went over with the rocks.

She managed to make it in one piece to homeroom, right as the bell rang. Everyone was already seated and she pulled out her digiTeacher Controller to take rollcall. Only Jonny and Lucy were missing. Jonny hadn't been back since last week because he was out with the flu. Lucy never missed class, and she was never late. *Maybe she went to the bathroom or was running an errand for another teacher?*

"Has anyone seen Lucy Gamble today?" Catherine asked, with no response from the class. They all looked like they just woke up and hadn't slept very well. Some even had crust in their eyes from the sandman still, and a few were sleeping! One Chinese student, Peter Liang, appeared to be not only sleeping, but drooling down the side of his shirt. She made a little knock on her desk and cleared her throat to try to wake the sleepers. They barely moved. Only Peter woke up, just to wipe his face on his sleeve and then put his head down on his desk to go back to sleep. Another student in the back, Tracy Brooker, had a small mirror out and was picking at zits, hoping that it would be hidden by her long hair hanging down on both sides of her face.

"I see that everyone is ready and excited for the day. Let's check the events. Ah, we have a pep rally today," she said and was met with groans and rolling of eyes from nearly everyone awake. "Are any of you participating in the show?" She had completely forgotten about the pep rally herself. Usually they put on a good show here at Desert Grande High School. The dance team, band, glee club and drama club all taking turns or working together to bring out school spirit.

"Not if we can help it," mumbled Jack Fairchild, while looking into his digiStudent Notebook. He was a quiet student who normally didn't speak in class, and was fairly withdrawn. He was always doing his homework on his Notebook during class and it looked like he never paid attention. Somehow, despite the lack of attention in class, he always managed to get good grades. He looked up from his Notebook, surprised he had said anything aloud himself.

Everyone looked so down and out, even more so than a typical Wednesday. "It looks like you could all use a pep rally. The comradery, the coming together to support each other, creates bonds and improves morale. I know the academic decathlon team that is going to nationals will appreciate the cheers and support. Plus, you get to leave fourth period early," Catherine said with as must gusto as she could muster this early in the morning. They got to leave fourth period early, but that meant her lunch break was extra short today and she was hoping to meet with Anthony as soon as possible to warn him about ... *What, a cyborg telling her in a dream he was sick and needed penicillin??* The thought was so ridiculous, but she still sensed Anthony might be in danger and wouldn't be able to live with herself if something happened to him.

She felt her armband pulse and looked down to find Anthony had texted back, "Sure, 11:30, park near mine. You bringing lunch?" Her heart jumped. She would have to skip the pep rally, and probably be late for her next class, and now she needed to pick up lunch too! She punched in the route into her navigation and searched to try to figure-out where she would get food on the way from the school to the mine. There weren't many restaurants that way. She started looking up meal options that were available and then she got another text. The strange number that had texted her earlier finally responded, "Jordan Muntz. I'm outside your door."

How did he get my number? Catherine thought. "Class, I'll be right back," she said as she turned the north wall to News Channel 4 and slipped out the door. No one even looked up, half were snoring.

"We need to talk," Jordan almost commanded as he grabbed Catherine by the arm and moved her away from her homeroom door and into a side hallway. His grip was very tight, and he looked like he hadn't brushed his hair or shaved today. "What did you get me into?" he demanded.

"What do you mean?" Catherine responded, completely shocked by his appearance and question. She pulled her arm from his grip and said, "How could I have gotten you into something? You look terrible. Did you even shower this morning?"

"The older brother from the article I gave you yesterday, he was in my dream last night. Except, like you said he had changed, he looked, walked, moved like he was a machine. Or, at least partially a machine. At first, he just stared at me with those golden eyes of his and then disappeared. Then he comes back just to put his arm through my chest, rip out my heart and begin to laugh maniacally as he squeezed my heart to a bloody pulp in front of my face. I get the distinct impression he doesn't like me," Jordan declared, emphatically.

Catherine had to stop herself from laughing, or even smiling though she thought the entire thing was funny. *Macho Jordan, upset over a dream?* "It was just a dream, Jordan, pull yourself together," she finally managed to get out.

Jordan was not amused. And quite frankly, it was hilarious to see such a tough guy upset over something so silly as a dream. He opened his mouth to say something then looked at Catherine putting her hand over her mouth to hide her smile and then he stopped. Sulking, with his normal grumpy demeanor, he said, "I would think that you of all people would understand."

"It isn't real; it is just a dream," Catherine tried to reassure him, but it just seemed to turn his mood darker. Okay, Jordan was not handling this very well. Maybe he wasn't used to having nightmares.

"Not real? That was the most real dream I have ever had! I did some more research yesterday. This guy Daniel Jahren and his family buried their research, and their research facility to hide something. He and his brother are supposed to be dead. Dead! How is he in our dreams? And how did he find me? Did you tell him about me?" Jordan asked.

Daniel was dead? That didn't make any sense. "I might have mentioned you in my dream last night. I think I spoke highly of you though. I said you were the only one who knew the truth that I could trust," Catherine answered, trying to recall the details of her dream. She couldn't remember everything; it was a dream, after all.

"I know the truth? Great! I don't know the truth. But I bet I know more than you, else you would be scared like me right now. I need to show you my research. You obviously have no idea what is going on, or refuse to believe what is right in front of your face. This is real, Catherine, it isn't just a dream. Is nothing real to you? You need to see what I have found. Can you come by my place after school today?" Jordan requested.

"I have so much grading ..." Catherine was trying to form excuses to not be alone with Jordan. She didn't know what would happen between them after the hiking trip when he mentioned he would go "camping" with her anytime. She was loyal to Anthony and she was sure he wouldn't want her alone at Jordan's place either. But, really she was curious about the research he had done and wanted to make him feel better; he was obviously very upset. She finally said, "I guess I can probably make it if I hold off grading a few essays. Text me your address later."

Jordan looked slightly less gloomy as he quickly headed back towards his classroom. She caught herself rubbing her arm where Jordan had gripped her; he had been so upset he probably left a bruise. *By a dream?* She had been dealing with Cyborg Daniel showing up in her dreams for months and it didn't bother her too much. *Maybe knowing that he was real hadn't fully sunk in? Was she in some sort of denial state? What did Jordan know that she didn't?*

"Taking a break, Miss Newton?" said Principal Repalle. His voice made Catherine jump away from the wall she had been leaning on and spin around to see him standing not three feet away.

"I'm sorry, sir, I just ... was heading to the bathroom," Catherine lied as best she could.

"You look like you have been sleeping better. Have you been having any more bad dreams?" he inquired.

Catherine was taken back for a second. She had forgotten that she had mentioned her dreams to Mr.

Repalle. *What had she said?* "Yes, I still seem to be disturbed by the rumbling from the mines. That man keeps visiting my dreams and telling me to 'close the mine.' Ridiculous, right?"

"Well, we don't want that, do we? I mean, if the mine closed, what would happen to this town? We would have to close down the school. You don't want to be re-assigned, do you, Miss Newton?" Mr. Repalle said. He let the message sink in, then he walked away with his signature phrase, "Good day."

Catherine decided to head towards the bathroom, just to add a little substance to her lie and maybe splash some cold water on her face. She walked into the bathroom and heard some weak sobbing in the far stall. There were small sneakered feet, pigeon-toed and pointing down, that abruptly picked up off the floor. Whomever it was, they didn't want to be seen.

"Hello. I know you're in there. Are you okay?" Catherine queried, tentatively.

The sneakered feet dropped back down and the door slowly swung open. It was Lucy peering back through teary green eyes and wiping off wet cheeks. "Miss Newton? I am sorry I was not in homeroom," she said as she started to cry again.

"It is okay, Lucy. It is just homeroom. I am sure with your merit level you can miss a few homerooms with no consequence," Catherine responded as she took some paper towels to dab on Lucy's cheeks. "What's going on?"

"I'm just not feeling well. My head is pounding and my mind is racing. I finished all my homework for the entire week yesterday afternoon. I haven't been able to sleep either," replied Lucy.

"Well, have you been by the nurse's office?" asked Catherine, concerned.

"Yes, Nurse Betty Green said I was fine. She offered me two aspirin but I haven't taken them yet … I just don't like taking pills," Lucy answered.

"Well, aspirin has been known to help with headaches, Lucy. You said your head was pounding, right? Two aspirin is pretty safe. How about we take that aspirin and get back to class? If you are still not feeling well we can go back to the nurse's office and insist on a more thorough check-up, okay?" Catherine offered.

"Okay, Miss Newton. If you think it will help," Lucy said as she pulled the aspirin out of her pocket and went over to the sink to get some water to drink the pills down.

"Good. I will walk you back to class and I will mark you as here this morning in homeroom. Does that make you feel better?" Catherine asked as she held Lucy's hair back to drink the water from the sink. Lucy nodded emphatically, water spilling down her lips. She seemed a bit flushed, and Catherine could feel the heat radiating from her forehead. Her eyes could be seen much better in the bright light above the sink. They looked different, her pupils were very tiny and it made her already large eyes look even larger.

As they walked out of the bathroom, the bell for class was ringing and students started pouring out of the nearby rooms. Lucy was off in what was likely the direction of her next class before Catherine could even take a step forward into the passing throng. *I guess she didn't need that homeroom mark on her Notebook,* Catherine thought as she headed to her classroom.

As she was walking towards her class she got a buzz on her phone band on her arm. She tried to ignore it so that she didn't trip over another student. She hurried to her classroom. When she arrived, she first had to turn off the news channel. Next, she had to put up the questions for the reading assignment today. Finally safely at her desk, she looked down to see that the buzz had been a message from Anthony saying he got called into a meeting and couldn't make lunch. He asked if they could meet after work.

"Sure" she replied, "same place?"

And he texted back immediately, "Yes, 5ish."

Great. It was going to be nerve-wracking waiting that long to talk to him, but she would have to power through. *Wait. She had to meet Jordan after work too!* Maybe Jordan could wait a bit later tonight, tomorrow even? She didn't like the idea of going over to his place after dark. She'd have to ask him at lunch, though she didn't think he was going to be very pleased based on his actions earlier.

Oh no, the pep rally! She realized the pep rally today would go through their normal lunch hour, and then she would likely not have time to catch Jordan before the end of the day. She would just have to make it over to him somehow, or text him, which just seemed too strange right now. And find lunch. Which reminded her, she had been so busy worrying about text messages this morning she had skipped breakfast too. She'd probably pass out if she didn't eat all day, so that was her Number One priority as soon as she could find a break.

Her normal empty fourth period was now a mad dash to the faculty lounge combinator to grab a meal and find Jordan before she had to be at the pep rally. Unfortunately, she wasn't the only faculty who had forgotten her lunch and the line was longer than she expected. Jordan was nowhere to be found. The line was barely moving. There was always the salad bar; that would be quick. Not hot, and not the scrumptious smelling pizza that was the special of the day, but it would work to keep her from passing out later. Catherine left the line and headed to the salad bar. She was able to sit and eat for a few minutes before the announcement came on the intercom for everyone to head over to the pep rally. She heard grumbles from the faculty who had stood in line the whole time and would now miss lunch.

As Catherine left the teacher's lounge she was almost run over by the band making their way to the gymnasium. The marching band also decided to start playing the school fight song right as they passed by and she had to duck to miss being hit by a crashing cymbal and then a bass drum hammer flying in the air towards her head.

Was she just accident-prone or where these kids trying to kill her? She couldn't decide. She kept a comfortable distance behind the band, just in case. Plus, the narrow hall made the sound of the band reverberate so loud it made the lockers shake. The clamor was enough to make anyone want to stay back. She continued to follow the band into the gymnasium, which was a mistake. She didn't realize that right behind her the dance team had formed and she was sandwiched in-between like Act Two in a three-act show. As they entered the gym, all she could think to do was smile and wave like a celebrity. Then she quickly walked over to the bench area where the other teachers had gathered. She was sure that she was blushing red the entire time, and that gave it away that she wasn't supposed to be there, plus she could see Elisabeth almost doubled over laughing.

She watched as the dance team came out into formation, kicking in unison until the drum rolls from the band that had formed into a block behind them stopped. The band began to play one of the Top 40 songs on the radio, something by someone named Jazzy Duke. The song was about club crawling or beer hoping or something. The hip gyrations from the young girls seemed highly inappropriate and the tuba players behind them swayed back and forth heavily, with hip thrusts at key emphasizing phrases in the song. When the show was over, Principal Repalle came down to the center of the open gym with a microphone to announce the decathlon team. A small group of students in black blazers with gold insignia arose and began filing down from the center of the stands, high fiving everyone on their way.

Lucy Gamble was one of the students in uniform who were gathering next to Principal Repalle at the center of the gym. She was the only one Catherine recognized besides a very tall student, Edward Paulson, from her fifth period, who usually had a very relaxed disposition. Apparently, this was the best decathlon team in the state four years running and everyone was excited to kick off this year in the same direction. A teacher she didn't know very well, Linda Trego, was obviously their advisor, given her presence below and the absolute look of pride and exuberance she had on her well made-up face. She looked like she belonged in the '90s, and was attempting a pure Madonna knockoff from head to toe.

As Mrs. "Madonna" Trego began to introduce each student, Catherine could see Lucy looking more and more pale. By the time it was Lucy's turn to take the microphone and say a few words, her hands were visibly shaking. She reached out to take the mic and immediately dropped to the floor and began convulsing. Catherine ran straight to her and could see blood coming out of the young girl's eyes, ears and nose. Lucy's forehead was burning hot. Catherine couldn't help but think of her dream last night. *Could Lucy be exposed to the same infection as Anthony, the one that Daniel had described?* There was no time to guess. She pointed to Edward Paulson and told him to get ice and then asked Nurse Betty for as much penicillin as she could find, especially shots. Catherine told everyone to stand back and out of the way as she turned Lucy on her side so she wouldn't choke on her tongue from the convulsions.

Edward came back quickly and they placed the ice all around Lucy's neck and under her head. Nurse Betty was running in heels as fast as her little feet could click away, carrying several large syringes, yelling "I'm coming! I'm coming!" down the hallway. She seemed to be taking forever so Catherine got up and met her in the hallway, grabbing the syringes from Betty and running them back the rest of the way to Lucy. When she got to Lucy, she suddenly realized she had no idea what to do with the needles.

"Gluteus Maximus!" yelled Nurse Betty still running to get to the center of the gym.

"Stick her in the butt!" a student yelled and was met by giggles that were quickly subdued by the stern look of Principal Repalle.

Oh right, the largest muscle group was the glutes, in the posterior. Catherine injected Lucy as fast as she could with as many of the syringes, making her right hip look like a pin cushion.

"One of those was Tylenol to help bring down the fever. What made you think she needed penicillin?" asked the nurse as she dabbed the blood from Lucy's face.

Lucy had stopped convulsing and was staring straight ahead, pupils as tiny as pin pricks. If it wasn't for the high speed at which Lucy was breathing, she would look like a rock because she was so stiff.

"I ... I ... um ... don't know," replied Catherine as she brushed back Lucy's hair and tried to think of what to say next. She looked up, everyone was staring at her. "I've seen this before," she finally said, then added, "I think it would be wise to give everyone who was in close contact with Lucy today penicillin as well, just to be safe."

Principal Repalle immediately gathered the decathlon team and their horrified advisor. "Has anyone else been in contact with this young lady?" No one in the gymnasium said a word; you could have heard a pin drop. He followed up with, "Teachers, please ensure all students are back in their class as soon as possible, as orderly as possible. Demerits should be given for any stragglers. Everyone, please head to your fourth period. Good day."

"How much penicillin do you have left, Mrs. Green?" asked the principal.

"That was everything I had. I will have to call in some from the hospital. They are pretty quick and they are on their way already. In the meantime, I think it is best to keep this small group quarantined. Let's bleach all our clothes to be safe. We'll all have to change into gym clothes for the day until they are done. That includes shoes and socks," replied Nurse Betty Green.

"You don't expect us to bleach the BLACK decathlon jackets do you? The gold embroidery is going to fray in those industrial machines. It will ruin our team!" yelled Linda Trego. "My lace jacket will never make it! It will be destroyed! And my gloves!"

"Now, now, Mrs. Trego, it is only clothes. It is what is in the team's heads and not what they wear that the judges are interested in for the decathlon," Mr. Repalle said as soothingly as possible to a frantic Linda who looked like she was about to have a nervous breakdown.

Lucy began to grumble and sit up, ice chips falling all around her. She looked down and saw the needles sticking out of her leg and began to scream.

"Lie down, dear, you've been through a lot," the nurse cautioned as she pulled the needles out of her leg. Seeing the needles must have been the last straw for Lucy, because she then fainted into the pile of ice chips.

Even though she had just fainted, Catherine was relieved to see Lucy doing better. She looked calm, her breathing was easy and the bleeding had long stopped. It looked like the penicillin and ice was the right call. And that made Catherine worry about Anthony. He could be convulsing on a floor right now somewhere and she couldn't even get to him until after work. She would have to swipe an extra shot of penicillin to bring to Anthony when the syringes showed up from the hospital. She just hoped she could get it to him in time.

CHAPTER 10

Sunset on the Valley

At the last bell, Catherine tried to find Jordan to let him know she couldn't meet him tonight but he was long gone and she didn't want to linger in the halls too long. She felt more than uncomfortable running around the school in nothing more than gym shorts, a school T-shirt, and tennis shoes. She filled out the shorts a little too well and her long bare legs were not something students were used to seeing. She had to yell at a few small groups of pubescent boys for ogling. She passed by Mrs. Trego, who was still crying over ruined clothing, and said her condolences. She couldn't help but notice Linda was wearing an extra-large school gym shirt that she had rolled the sleeves up and ripped on the side to make a bow tie. *This lady was obsessed with '90s fashion!*

Catherine decided she would just have to text Jordan, sending him "Can't meet tonight, rain check?" before heading out to the park near the mine to meet up with Anthony. It was freezing outside and the laundry was still not done. She rummaged through her car and found a long sweater in the trunk that would have to do and put the extra penicillin shot in the pocket. It had not been easy to get, and she had to lie and say they had miscounted earlier when giving everyone shots. She wasn't sure, but Principal Repalle had given her a look and she thought that he might have suspected something. She didn't care; she needed to get the shot to her boyfriend or he could die.

Catherine texted Anthony to let him know she was on her way, and it worried her that she hadn't heard from him since the earlier text when he changed the plans to later today. While she was staring at her phone band, a text came back from Jordan, "Tonight, no rain checks."

Urgh! So, she would have to deal with eccentric Jordan tonight. It had been too long of a day already. *He was freaking out about dreaming of a cyborg? Really?* She had been dreaming of Daniel Jahren and his golden eyes and jerking mechanical movements for months now. It wasn't a big deal. It was just a dream. Of course, he never threatened to kill her in her dreams. *But, it is just a dream and you can't kill someone in a dream, you can't even hurt them! Jordan had his heart ripped out and he was fine, didn't he realize that?* He probably just needed someone to listen to him. He seemed like such a lonely guy.

"Okay, late date w Anthony," texted Catherine, telling the truth but also trying to remind him she had a boyfriend. She waited a few minutes for a reply, nothing came back from Jordan.

She looked out into the desert around her. There were large dark clouds on the horizon to the east. A storm was brewing and would probably come in tonight. Most of the sky was clear and the distant sun was beginning to turn the fringes to a dusty red. She felt chills as she looked out into the expanse. Something felt different about the day that she couldn't quite wrap her mind around.

The car pulled itself up to the park near the mine and she put it in manual to find a parking spot near some picnic benches. That reminded her, *she had forgotten to grab anything to eat on the way!* She sat in her car shivering, looking at dinner options she could pick up near the area when Anthony would eventually arrive and want food.

Three tiny knocks on her window made her sit straight up and almost jab herself with the shot of penicillin in her pocket that she had been absent-mindedly fondling. Anthony was outside her window smiling with a big handsome grin. She jumped out of the car and gave him a big hug. She had to move her face quickly out of the way when he reached to kiss her lips.

"Here, you have to take this!" Catherine proclaimed as she straightaway handed Anthony the syringe, pushing him back.

"What is it?" Anthony asked, looking down at the needle in confusion.

"It is a shot of penicillin. There is something going around and I think you might have caught something," she said.

"How would I have caught something?" Anthony looked worried.

Right then her armband vibrated and a text message from Jordan with his address and "Tonight!" popped up on her screen.

"Is there something I should know?" Anthony asked.

"I had a dream you were sick. Then this little girl at school today got sick the same way as you had in my dream. They used penicillin on her and she got better and I just thought it couldn't hurt to give you some too so I got this from the nurse," Catherine said as she cleared her text messages from her screen. She had spent all day coming up with that lie so she didn't have to tell him about dreaming of cyborgs.

"Well, that is odd. You see, the reason why I couldn't come to lunch today was that I was brought in to get a shot of penicillin from the on-call doctor at work. He said he noticed something in my last physical and they wanted to make sure I was in great shape, and they said that they want to take good care of me at the mine ... Are you sure there isn't something you need to tell me?" he asked, looking down at Catherine's arm band. He had apparently noticed the text from Jordan.

"No. I mean one of my co-workers wants me to come over tonight and discuss some history about the mines and viruses ... he is a bit paranoid, full of conspiracy theories. I promised him I would hear him out," replied Catherine.

"Him? And you don't think it is inappropriate for you to meet a male co-worker at his house at night, alone?" inquired Anthony, crossing both arms in front of his massive chest.

"It is, I am sorry. I will cancel, look, right now ..." Catherine said as she texted back Jordan to let him know she couldn't make it. Anthony was frowning, but he looked satisfied with the text, for now.

"You look cold. What are you wearing?" he asked, checking out her gym clothes.

"Oh, that little girl that I mentioned who almost died today during the pep rally, Lucy Gamble, had an infectious bacterium. Everyone around her when she went into convulsions and was bleeding had to have their clothes bleached and had to change into school gym clothes," Catherine replied. "I was one of the few who were right next to her when she got sick, so I lost my clothes to the laundry machine."

"Lucy Gamble? That wouldn't be Forman Gamble's daughter?" Anthony asked.

"Yes, I believe she is his daughter, why?" Catherine replied. Anthony looked pale.

"Monday, a man died in convulsions on the floor and Forman Gamble was there ..." started Anthony.

"And so were you?" interrupted Catherine, eyes wide, everything was coming together. That must have been how Anthony had gotten exposed to the bacterium.

"Yes. Lets walk for a minute, it will warm you up," Anthony said as he pulled Catherine's sweater around her, slid the syringe in her pocket and put his hand on the small of her back to lead her down the trail towards a large canyon overpass bridge.

Anthony stopped when they got to the center of the bridge and he said, "Catherine, there is something going on at the mine. We aren't just finding rocks down there ..."

"Viruses? Like the lake viruses? Is that what you are finding? Jordan said that there were people from the mine in white suits at the lake on Saturday," Catherine interjected. *Was Jordan right about the viruses? Was Daniel?*

"Jordan said, huh? I don't know. All I know is that I was brought somewhere that I didn't know existed on

Monday after the incident with the old man that died. It had to be ten stories below the shed, a lab. They threatened my family, Catherine. They knew about you too, that we had come to the mine together to get my phone band and had explored the tunnels. If Lucy almost died, that means they are not as in control as they want us to believe. Whatever is going on, I don't think we are safe ... I need to keep my family safe," Anthony said, looking flustered.

Catherine was in shock. *A hidden facility at the mine where they hid viruses?* Now this was more than just a coincidence. *Was everything from her dreams going to end up being real?*

"What are you going to do, Anthony?" Catherine asked. He had never looked so shaken. He stood there looking out into the red sunset, black clouds coming out of the east. There was a distant rumble, and a flash that lit up the canyon.

"Do you think they will re-assign us to the same place?" Anthony at last asked, looking down at Catherine. His dark look had changed to one of love and hope, and he continued with, "They will re-assign us together if we are married."

"What are you implying? Why would they re-assign us?" Catherine barely got out as she watched Anthony get to one knee and pull out a ring. It had a beautiful, heart-shaped ruby that was cupped in golden hands. *He was proposing, now?!?*

"What do you mean re-assign us?" Catherine asked again. She was trying not to look at the ring, as if that would make the whole situation disappear if she didn't acknowledge the ring.

"Will you marry me, Catherine? I couldn't stand to lose you," Anthony asked.

"Lose me? I … I can't. We have only been dating a few months, Anthony. This is just too fast." Catherine was surprised at herself, she had said it: it was too fast. But what was he planning to do that would lead to them re-assigning them?

"I know it is soon, but you are the best it is ever going to get for me and I know it. From the day I met you, I knew you were the one," Anthony said, still looking up holding the ring, in hope that she would say yes.

"I just can't, Anthony. Please, it is too soon," Catherine explained.

"I understand," he said in the end, getting up from the ground.

"I'm so sorry," she pleaded. Her chest was starting to hurt. It felt like they were breaking up and she wanted to cry.

"Then I hope we get re-assigned to the same place, or that you can wait for me," he said brushing the tears from her cheek with his big fingers.

"What are you planning to do, Anthony? Please don't say you are going to do something to the mine … are you?" she inquired, hoping she was wrong.

"They threatened my family, they threatened you. That old man didn't die of a stroke. What they are doing, playing around with viruses and bacteria in secret, it just isn't right and it needs to stop. I can stop them. I should have sooner. I feel like a coward," he replied. "You know they offered me a promotion? And that is all I was thinking about ... Is Lucy Gamble okay?"

"Yes, we got her ice and penicillin immediately and she recovered fairly quickly," Catherine said.

"I am glad no one died. They must have known she was sick and let her go to school. How could they have let her into the school to infect others like that? They need to be stopped," he insisted, working himself up.

"I don't think they knew she was sick," Catherine started, then struggled to think of how to explain that she was the one who knew what to do with Lucy.

"What do you mean? They knew Forman Gamble and I were exposed. They gave us both penicillin today and asked us if we had any contact with anyone since the incident. So, they knew he went home to his family," he said.

"Well, they might not have known it would spread so fast or affect her the way it did ... see I was the one that treated her. Like I said, I had a dream last night, and you were in it. That is why I wanted to meet you for lunch, to tell you what happened ..."

"Do you dream about me often?" he asked, blushing, probably thinking about the naughty things he had done in his dream the night before.

"Umm, well, I have been having these warning dreams, about the mine. See, this man keeps telling me that it is dangerous and needs to be closed. Last night he told me you were infected and needed to be treated with penicillin. He told me all about the bacterium and how it works and when Lucy showed the exact signs he was talking about I knew what to do to save her life," Catherine explained, thankful to finally get it all out.

"I see. Do you think it is Jesus you are dreaming about?" Anthony asked, sincerely.

Catherine tried not to laugh. She knew he was serious. The idea that a golden-eyed cyborg was Jesus Christ in any way was too funny. "No, if anything, this man seems dangerous himself." Anthony just stood there, looking out into the canyon below and back towards the mine.

"Anthony, what are you planning to do? Should we go to the police, tell them what you saw?" she questioned.

"The police would never believe me. I am not sure I believe me," he said. "Besides, no one in this town wants the mine to shut down."

Catherine was shivering and trying to rub her arms to generate a bit of friction. The sun was set and the temperature had dropped a few more degrees.

"You need to get home, get into some warm clothes and get some rest. It sounds like you had a rough day," he told her as he hugged her close and rubbed her arms to generate frictional heat.

"I will be fine. I am worried about you. I don't want you to do anything dangerous," she insisted.

"I will only do what is right, and what needs to be done to protect my family," he said as he held her and led her down the path back to the car. She kept trying to think of what to say to stop him. But, from everything she knew about him, once he put his mind to something there was no changing it.

As he put her into her car, and set her destination, he whispered one last thing that sent chills to her bones: "I hope to see you again one day, my love." Then he pressed the autopilot and shut the door.

Catherine couldn't believe it. What was happening? One minute she was thinking she was going to save his life with this shot of penicillin, the next it seemed he was going to put that life in danger to shut down the mine. And she could do nothing to stop him! Well, nothing short of warning the cops, or Mr. Repalle could call his brother and ... what? Shoot Anthony?

She sat there, stunned, in her car while it drove her to the coordinates Anthony had set, which was her house. A vibration woke her from her stupor. Her armband was buzzing again, and it was Jordan, insisting that she meet him now. After a minute of contemplation, she decided to put in Jordan's address instead of her own into the navigation system. *Maybe Jordan could help her figure out what to do about Anthony?* She let him know she was on her way.

The car ran down a long, winding, upward road and into denser and denser trees on a hillside just east of the mine. The path became rough, and the road had turned to gravel a mile back before the car finally pulled up to a log cabin. The cabin had only one dim porch light on and a second light coming from the living room window. Everything else was pitch black all around, and there wasn't another house or street light for at least five miles. The place was secluded and dark, somewhat like Jordan himself.

Jordan opened the door and came out onto the porch with a small lantern to greet Catherine as she climbed the stairs.

"You actually came," he said, letting her into his house.

"Yes, I was with Anthony. He didn't want me to come here. He didn't think it was appropriate and I agreed with him so that is why I texted you I couldn't come earlier," she replied as she walked through the door into the warm living room with a log fire going in the fireplace. Besides the fireplace, the room was stark and bare, with only a recliner, small table and a TV. The back wall behind the recliner was made of a stack of books. Definitely the home of a reclusive, bookworm bachelor.

"What made you change your mind?" he asked as he handed her a drink that smelled and tasted like mulled wine.

"I think Anthony is going to do something dangerous tonight. I think he might blow up the mine!" she replied.

"What? Why?" Jordan exclaimed.

"He thinks that they are working on viruses in a deep underground lab and that it is dangerous. He said they threatened his family," she replied as she sat down cross-legged on the floor next to the fire to get warm, sipping on the wine.

"Well, that is what I wanted to talk to you about," Jordan said as he sat across from her in his recliner. "They *are* working on viruses at the mine. But not ones Greggo Sands made themselves, ones they are finding from an old facility that was buried in late 2017. And, before that, the viruses they were working on wiped out this whole area twice before. These are very dangerous viruses that have been linked to this town since before there was a town. I was doing some research on it all, and I finally put it together. Those brothers, the ones that are 'sleeping' as you say, in your dream. Well, they were part of experiments that dug up things here many years ago. And they buried themselves to try and stop the things they found," Jordan replied in grave tones.

"And you had to have me over tonight to tell me that?" Catherine asked.

"Well, I couldn't just tell you at school during lunch for Elisabeth to hear and spread all over town that I am a whack-job. Plus, I only came in today to talk to you. After the dream I had last night, I know they can't contain what they are doing at the mine. I plan on boarding up and riding this out right here, a safe distance from contamination. I have enough provisions for two to last a few years. It is manageable."

"So that is your solution, hole up and hide from it all?" Catherine replied. She was starting to feel a bit tipsy and noticed her speech was slurring.

"Yes, it worked for me last time during the dust. This will be no different," he explained.

"Whas in this drink, manitisss stoong ..." was the last thing Catherine remembered saying. And, as her vision went from blurry to black her last image was of Jordan quickly catching her before her head hit the fireplace.

When she finally opened her eyes again, she found her wrists tied together and attached to a bed headboard by a knot. She was lying in a bed covered in a large flannel blanket. She was still in her gym clothes underneath the blanket, thankfully fully clothed. The room was dark but when she rolled over she could see

Jordan, asleep next to her. She kicked him sharply with her left leg; he must have forgotten to tie her up completely.

"What are you thinking, you crazy paranoid idiot!" she screamed, trying to get a few more good shots in with her feet as he wrestled her down.

"This is for your own safety, Catherine! They have no idea what they are doing with those viruses. I am trying to help you!" he yelled as he held down her legs.

"This is crazy, Jordan. You can't just kidnap someone!" she screamed.

"I don't want to be alone," he said. "Last time, I had to watch my parents die and then I was alone for years before they found me. I don't want to be alone again. I can't be alone again."

"I'm sorry, Jordan, but this just isn't the way to make friends, okay? You could have just asked me to stay here, you know," she declared.

"I don't want just a friend. I know you feel it too. Deep down. I think you'd want to stay here with me. You just have to give it time, and we don't have time. So, I had to do something," he insisted.

"Jeeze. What is it with men!" Catherine professed. "Jordan, please let me go. I need to stop Anthony, and I was hoping you would help me; I'm afraid he will blow up the mine."

"No, he has chosen his fate and I hope he gets buried with the mine like the Jahrens did," Jordan replied.

"Jordan, please let me go," Catherine asked softly. "I promise we can talk. Just untie me."

"No. We can talk tomorrow. And if you kick me again I will tie up your feet too. Goodnight," he said as he turned over and tried to sleep.

"They will wonder were I am tomorrow at work. They can track my car, my phone, my texts with your address ... they will find me here. You will have to let me go, eventually," Catherine added.

"Not if everyone is dead, they won't notice," Jordan remarked, still turned away and trying to sleep.

"Why would everyone be dead? No one has died, except the old man yesterday anyway ... Look, the bacteria that killed him and made Lucy sick isn't that deadly and is treatable with penicillin. You are overreacting," Catherine replied.

"That bacteria was nothing, and it is only one of the many things they have buried in those labs the mine is trying to get into. I saw what these viruses can do. Daniel showed me after he ripped out my heart. There is no stopping that mining company from digging, which means they are going to open up Pandora's box any day now and it will be a long time before anyone goes looking for you. Especially now, with Anthony off to blow up the mine. I am not overreacting."

He stopped talking for a minute and took a few deep breaths then continued with, "Look, if your boyfriend manages to blow up the mine and stop it all, I will let you go as soon as we know none of the viruses escaped. Deal?" Jordan asked.

"No, no deal. I want to be let go now! I don't want Anthony to blow up the mine and I don't want to lay around here for days waiting for everyone in the town to die!" Catherine exclaimed.

"Too bad. Goodnight." Jordan responded, nonchalantly.

What in the world was with this guy? Was he really fully convinced that any day now viral Armageddon was going to be unleashed? She lay there staring at the impressive knot on the bedframe and the tie job around her wrist. He must have been a Boy Scout. Her father had taught her a thing or two about knots though, and she was prepared with teeth to rip the tie to shreds if she had to when he finally fell asleep.

She lay there waiting to hear him snore, which he never did. However, his breathing became regular and he seemed pretty still. She began to slowly pull at the rope until it began to slide free, one knot down. He had been pretty thorough. She began on the second knot and felt movement to her left, suddenly she saw a hand over the knot.

"Impressive. I was trying to keep you comfortable, but it looks like you want to be difficult," Jordan said as he pulled her hands above her head and re-tied the knot. "Goodnight," is all he said as he turned over once again to go to sleep.

Great! She was really stuck now! Jordan had fallen asleep already, confident in his knot. Catherine lay there wondering how the heck she was going to get free in time to stop Anthony, and if there was anyway of stopping him at all.

CHAPTER 11

Blowing up the Mine

Anthony knew one thing, how to blow something up. That is all he had been doing the last four years at the mine. He also knew how to get explosives and exactly where he wanted to put them. What he didn't know was how he was going to do all of that and not get caught before he executed his plan. There were cameras everywhere and guards at all times. He knew he had to wait until the guard was lowest, right after 2 a.m. when there was a shift change. He also wanted no casualties. He couldn't live with himself if he knew he had murdered someone. Most importantly, for the plan to work, he needed access to the labs. As far as he knew, there was only one person that could get him into everywhere he needed to go tonight.

"Dr. Steinman, thank you for agreeing to see me," Anthony said as he reached out to shake the doctor's hand. They were outside the main entrance to the shed, where Dr. Steinman had just opened the door to let Anthony into the building.

"Anytime, that is what I am here for. I am sorry you are still not feeling well. You said your head hurt? Are you running a temperature?" the doctor asked.

"Yes. I think I might have a fever, and my head is pounding," Anthony answered as he slid inside the door. The doctor was busy locking the door behind him and Anthony could easily get to the belt Dr. Steinman wore around his waist that controlled the elevators and all of the entry points. Of course, Anthony had no idea what the access codes where, so it was no use getting to the belt without "convincing" the doctor to help him. He had to wait until the right time, where there were no cameras watching.

A tall, thin woman with short, slicked-back, strawberry-blonde hair and a stoic face walked up to greet them as they entered the lab below. She didn't say a word as she walked beside Dr. Steinman as they all headed towards one of the steel-doored rooms. Suddenly, she jabbed the doctor in the neck with a syringe and held onto his back, releasing the liquid into his vein. He spun around and punched upwards into her arm that was holding the syringe while using his other hand to push her whole body away by her throat. She flew back against the wall, bashing her head, and was instantly knocked out. The doctor pulled the syringe from his neck and his eyes got really wide for a second as he looked at the half-emptied contents, then he fell to the ground himself. Anthony caught the doctor about halfway to the ground and gently placed him on his back. He checked for a pulse at the neck and put his head down, with his ear to the doctor's mouth, listening for breathing. Nothing: no pulse, no breath. *She had killed him! But why?* He emptied out the syringe onto the doctor's jacket; it was just a clear liquid that smelled a bit acidic.

Anthony walked over to where the lady had landed and checked her pulse and breathing. She was still alive, just knocked out. He sat her up against the wall, bracing her neck. He did not know what to do. She might attack him if he woke her up, but he couldn't just leave her. He decided to shake her a little bit, and she responded with reaching out and clutching both of his arms and screaming. Which, of course, made him jump backwards and scream himself.

"I'm sorry. I didn't mean to scare you, I am actually here to help you, Anthony," the lady claimed with her hands still up, open palms out to show she was unarmed with any more syringes. She had a thick Russian accent.

"He's dead. You killed him," was all Anthony could think to say.

"Yes, he was going to kill you. He has killed several people. I saved your life. I was actually sent here to investigate what has been going on and I came across some very disturbing evidence this afternoon. Here, look at his arms," she said as she lifted up his lab coat to reveal dark streaks running up his muscles. She opened up his shirt and revealed the same dark streaking. "Quinta virus. He has been conducting illegal experiments on himself and others, then destroying the evidence. I found the bodies earlier. I knew he would figure out why I was here soon and I would end up in one of those barrels too."

"Barrels? What barrels? Who are you? How do you know who I am?" Anthony asked in a barrage.

"Sasha Mikhailov, head of Research and Development for Greggo Sands," she said as she reached out to grab his hand. "I was sent here by Alluri Repalle himself, yesterday. And you are Anthony Grant, a simple miner who was in the wrong place at the wrong time yesterday when a member of your crew, a Mr. Theodore Grayson, died suddenly exposing you to a dangerous bacterial infection for which you were treated with penicillin earlier today," the woman said as she rubbed the back of her head and neck absently.

"So, you came out yesterday just to investigate the old man's death? I am not buying that you didn't know about the experiments going on down here," Anthony said. Her story just didn't add up.

"No, I came out here yesterday to find out why traces of viruses have been continuously found in the nearby lake. Mr. Grayson's death was accidental, and also the first and only non-mining related death that anyone in the company knew about. Until now. Let me show you something," she stated as she stood up and began to walk over to the doctor's body. She removed his belt and brought it with her as she walked down the hall. Anthony followed reluctantly.

Sasha directed him into the tubes, where she entered in a number into the doctor's belt and the tube sucked them upwards. They landed on a sparsely cemented room that opened out into a cave that was dimly lit with led lamps. The entire cave was full of stalagmites and stalactites. There were beacon-like ribbons running along the walls, with little bits of quartz jutting out in between. The sound and smell of a distant waterfall filled the air. Sasha guided him down into the darkness of the expansive cave until they came across a river inside. There were three barrels located along the cave wall near the river's edge.

"Look inside," was all she said as she pointed her flashlight at the barrels.

Anthony opened the lid and found the jumbled-up remains of a dark-haired, muscular, young man with black streaks along his skin. His bloodshot eyes were open on his disembodied head and he was staring straight back up. There was blood coming from his eyes, ears and mouth, similar to what he had seen on the old man when he had died yesterday.

"This man couldn't have been dead for very long," Anthony said as he closed the lid and opened the next barrel. Another dismembered young man, this one with no black streaks on his skin, lay inside. "Or this one," he added. He didn't know much about dead bodies, but from hunting he knew that they would start to rot pretty soon if left outside like this and these didn't smell at all.

"Yes, all three of these men were killed in the last 24-hours alone. Who knows how many were killed before now. He's been throwing the barrels into this river, which heads out into the lake after going down a waterfall. I suspect the lake is so deep that the barrels get pretty wedged-in when they fall down the waterfall, about 50 feet from here. Likely, the viruses have been escaping due to leakage from cracks or ...."

"Viruses leaking?" Anthony interrupted.

"Yes, viruses. During mining here about seven years ago, we came across a lab that had been buried. We found viruses that could be used to enhance physical attributes and health. Nothing deadly, nothing dangerous. However, it was outside the scope of the mine crew here and kept with another division. My division. The labs here were created because we needed quarantine areas in case we came across any other viruses that might not be so friendly. We also needed someone to handle the quarantine process, so we put Dr. Steinman in charge. We have found three labs and five viruses so far during mining activity in the area. However, Dr. Steinman has taken it upon himself to conduct more research than was authorized and I do not know how far it all goes. I do know that you would likely be in one of those barrels if I hadn't stopped him tonight," Sasha proclaimed.

"I am sorry, but it is hard to say thank you for saving my life when I feel like hiding viruses in the first place puts you on the wrong side of all of this as well," Anthony replied.

"I am not a murderer, I am a scientist!" Sasha exclaimed.

"Yet, you experiment with viruses that you know nothing about. Viruses that were developed by someone else that you know nothing about. You play god, and it is wrong," Anthony declared.

Sasha just looked at him as if he had just said the sky was made of Skittles.

"We need to stop the mining. These labs, these viruses, were buried for a reason and we have no right to dig them up," Anthony stated as matter-of-factly as he could, looking her dead in the eye to ensure she knew how serious he was as he took the belt that had belonged to the doctor out of her hands.

"What do you plan to do, Anthony?" she said, with her head turned sidewise and her eyes narrow. She looked like a bird inspecting a worm.

"I am going to blow up the mine," he replied, simply, as he walked over to the tubes. "You can help if you want."

"There are twelve stories of labs here, with over $1 billion in synthesized viral product ..." she began as she followed behind Anthony.

"So, you're killing people for money?" Anthony asked. He wasn't slowing down and was not deterred by her spouting figures of money.

"Are you willing to kill innocent people too?" she finally said when she saw he was un-phased.

"What do you mean? What people?" he demanded.

"I don't know how many people are here in quarantine. I don't know how far the deception goes and how many people were brought into the labs. Dr. Steinman had his own agenda; he had at least seventeen other test subjects that I knew about. Like I said, there are twelve stories of labs and quarantine rooms, and possibly people in those labs or rooms."

"Then we will have to go to each of the twelve stories and every single room and clear them all out. Maybe helping me clear this mess out will help you clear your conscience in working with deadly viruses and bacteria that you just found laying around and used to make money," he said as he looked down into her steel-grey eyes. Her scarlet cheeks and pouty lips indicated his message had gotten across.

"Alright, I will help you disable the mine. But, I do not want to blow the whole thing up. I hope that isn't what you expect to do, is it? Blow the whole thing up? Who knows what kind of backlash on the mountain that would have. We know we haven't uncovered everything that was buried here, and who knows what consequences that would have if those labs were to be disturbed. This has to be a controlled demolition," she demanded.

Anthony nodded his head in agreement. Of course he planned a controlled explosion. He knew exactly what to do to close off each of the passages and disable the lifts in the shed. He looked down at the belt in his hands and suddenly realized that his original plan would never have worked without the help of Sasha. He had no idea how to work this belt, what numbers to press to open rooms, elevators, or anything. He had known that, and had planned to force the doctor to enter the required keys. But, he hadn't realized until now he would have had to twist the doctor's arm pretty hard to get him through a twelve-story facility to search for people.

"It is going to be a long night. Let's start from the bottom," Sasha said as she punched the code into her belt that sent both of them rocketing downward into the tubes.

~ ~ ~

Catherine must have fallen asleep waiting for Jordan to go to sleep again so she could work the binding on her hands. She was no longer at Jordan's, but was somehow standing in front of a red door with yellow reflective tape around the edges. She realized she was looking at the door she had entered when she and Anthony had snuck into the mine to get his phone band. She reached for the handle right as the door opened and Daniel walked out.

"What are you doing here, Catherine?" he asked. "Back for more exploring?"

"Exploring? No. I don't know how I got here or why. Actually, I didn't even mean to fall asleep. Last I remember, I was trying to work out the knot in the rope Jordan had tied me up with," she answered, honestly.

"Jordan! I told you he was trouble. I told you to stay away! You never listen, do you? Why does he have you tied up?" Daniel yelled as he punched the mountainside to his right and the rocks fell into a thousand pieces of shining dust at the impact. The whole cliffside was rumbling.

"It was an emergency. See, I came over to his house tonight to try and get him to help me stop Anthony from blowing up the mine," she explained. "Anthony has it in his head that is the only way to stop people from being killed around here and he is so hard headed, I didn't think I would be able to convince him to stop."

"Anthony wants to blow up the mine? Tonight? What do you mean blow up the mine?" Daniel demanded.

"I mean, I told him about you and my dreams finally and he thinks that it is not right and that the viruses need to remain buried. He is so stubborn! He thought you were Jesus ..." Catherine tried to think of how to explain Anthony to Daniel, and it seemed impossible.

"Oh, I am far from Jesus. I told you to stop the mining, not blow up the mine! Blowing up the mine is the last thing that needs to happen! It could destabilize the entire region! The mountainside has already suffered enough damage from when we buried our facilities," Daniel replied.

"So, you did purposefully bury yourself alive? Who would do that?" Catherine asked, stunned to find that everything that Jordan had told her was true. "Are you dead? Are you a ghost?"

"Ha! No, I am not a ghost!" he laughed, then paused for a minute, looking down into the valley. "I did it to stop the very thing your boyfriend may release tonight, something far more dangerous than you can imagine ..." he trailed off in thought, eyes flashing in strange symbols. "What are his plan?" Daniel finally asked.

"I don't know. Honestly, I am guessing that he is going to blow up the mine. I know his specialty is explosives, and I know he said he had to protect his family. Then he said something that made me think he thought he might never see me again and it scared me. He seemed sure to do something tonight, and I didn't know if I should stop him or how ... that is why I went to Jordan," Catherine explained. "I needed advice and he seems to be the only one who knows anything around here."

"That's right, you are currently tied up in the clutches of a mad man that you think you can trust. This Jordan. Why exactly has he tied you up?" Daniel was looking at her intently and he took another step forward and asked, "Has he done anything to you? Has he hurt you?"

"No, he drugged me with some wine and then tied me to his bed. He said he doesn't want to be alone when all the viruses get out and kill everyone. He hasn't hurt me; he just seems lonely," she replied. "I feel sorry for him, really."

"Most lonely men don't drug and kidnap people, Catherine. He is insane and you are in more danger than you know. So innocent. You should have listened to me ... Now, I am going to have to rescue you," he insisted.

Catherine laughed, "Rescue me? You are a dream, a figment of my imagination, you can't be real."

"I am real, Catherine, haven't you figured that out yet? Are you still in denial, after everything that has happened?"

"Okay, so say you are real. You said it yourself, you are asleep somewhere, buried I assume."

"I am real, Catherine." Daniel said gravely. "How exactly do you plan to escape Jordan's bedroom ... unscathed? He has dark plans for you, and you have no idea how much danger you are in. Is nothing real to you?"

"I will figure something out. And I will stop Anthony. I can manage. I don't need your help," Catherine declared. Somehow, the thought of Daniel awake and in the real world was more frightening than the idea of being stuck as a prisoner of Jordan's.

"Strong. Independent. I like it. Foolish. But I like it," Daniel laughed. "Your innocence is a gift, and a curse."

"I need to go, I need to get those ropes undone and get to Anthony before he blows up the whole mountainside," she replied.

"I will see you soon," Daniel said, with a smile and a sense of finality that was unnerving.

Catherine tried to ignore the knot in her stomach that was forming as she looked into his eyes. She closed her eyes and tried to concentrate on waking up. When she opened them again, she was in a dark room, hands tied up behind her head to a cast iron bedframe. It was still nighttime and Jordan was asleep next to her on the bed.

She began to wiggled her wrists to clear room in the ropes. She had pretty flexible wrists and was able to twist her right one backwards to catch hold of one of the three knots with her ring finger. It felt like hours, but she was finally able to get her left hand free. Once her left hand was free, she pulled the knot out of the bedpost holding her right hand and gently slipped off the edge of the bed.

She lay on the floor for a second, listening to Jordan's steady breathing. When she was sure he was still sound asleep, she slowly crawled along the floor on hands and knees towards where she hoped was the living room in the pitch-black house. The floors, along with everything else in the cabin, were all wood. The wood floor below creaked with the weight of her body and it sounded like gun blasts to her hears in contrast to the dead of the night. Her heart was beating so hard, the thuds in her ears sounded like canons to go along with the creaky gun blasts. She could barely see and used her hands to feel her way in the dark as best she could, trying not to knock anything over or run into something.

The lights came on and, in less than a second, she was being lifted into the air. She kicked as hard as she could, throwing her arms and head back at the same time. The movement knocked Jordan back and down to the floor. She managed to get behind his back, then yanked his left arm backwards while putting her knee on his spine. She used the rope that he had tied her up with to wrap around his arms and tie in a knot behind him. She was raised on a ranch in Montana; she used to rope calves for fun, and tying Jordan up proved even easier.

"Stay down, Jordan. I am going. I need to stop Anthony," she said as she got up to leave. He tried to stand up and she kicked him in the shin, knocking him down.

Jordan was writhing in pain on the floor but managed to get out, "You can't stop it. The viruses are coming and you will die if you don't stay with me!"

"Jordan, you are crazy. Goodbye," she replied as she escaped, seizing her phone band and purse off the counter and heading out the front door. She jumped into her car and turned it on in manual mode so she could immediately back out. She knew that rope wouldn't hold Jordan for long and wanted to get as far away as she could, as fast as she could. She turned around as she accelerated backward all the way along the gravel driveway. She then spun the car around as the road turned out to lead back down the hillside, throwing up rocks and mud everywhere.

The road was dark and desolate; there were no lights except from her car and she was driving like a mad woman. The twists and turns in the gravel caused the car to slide several times. It didn't help that there were potholes full of water all along the path down. The storm she had seen earlier at the park near the mine must have come through in the night while she was asleep because not only were the potholes full of water but there were several tree branches on the road.

Just as she was thinking about slowing down, there was a loud explosion. She instinctively turned left to look in the direction of the sound and the resulting swerve of the steering wheel caused the car to nearly go off the side of the road. She slammed the brakes and the tires slid 20 feet in the loose, muddy gravel. *The explosion, was it the mine?* she thought as she got out of her car to see if she could tell where the blast had come from. She looked in the direction she had heard the blast. All she could see was darkness all around and all she could hear was the sound of bullfrogs and crickets in the bushes next to the car. Something slithered on the ground at her feet and she jumped back in the car with a little yelp. *She hated snakes!* She took a few deep breaths while clutching the steer wheel.

Just as she started the car again and headed down the hill, another explosion rocked the hillside. This time, it knocked down a few boulders that began rolling towards her car. She hit the accelerator and dodged the rocks. She was busy navigating boulders, tree branches and potholes when another explosion slashed through the air and pounded the glass of her car with a loud bang.

This explosion was the strongest and it caused her car to bounce slightly down the gravel road. The road kept shaking after the blast, and the rumbling was getting louder. She looked in the rearview mirror and she could barely make it out, but it looked like everything she had passed earlier was coming down behind her. The rain from the midnight storm, and the explosions she had heard, must have triggered a landslide in the soggy hillside.

The last thing she remembered, she was hitting the accelerator to the floor and trying not to look at the mountain of trees, boulders and mud coming down behind her in the dim light of the rising sun.

CHAPTER 12

The Aftermath

Anthony couldn't believe it; he had done it! It helped that there ended up not being a single living person in the entire twelve floors of labs below the shed at the mine. After the first four floors, Sasha and he had split up the search: even floors for him and odd floors for her to inspect. She was waiting for him on the main floor of the shed when he was done with his search. They had found the explosives next, and planted them at the base of the elevators on the main floor of the shed first, to trap all entrances to the labs below.

The guards and miners working the night shift in the mine had to be cleared before the explosives could be set in the entrance. Sasha was instrumental in coming up with a way to get everyone out safely. She had hatched a plan to call a biohazard drill and get all of the minors out to the main yard where she could safely "quarantine" them while Anthony was able to go in and set the bombs needed down the corridors. She injected each of them with a serum Barbiturate mixture that would put them all to sleep quickly, so they couldn't go back into the mine before Anthony was finished.

Anthony set a 5-minute, timed detonation at the mine entrance and then headed back over to the shed to trigger the bombs there by a remote from a safe distance in the parking lot.

Everything had worked out perfectly, as planned. Anthony was sitting in his car, looking out at the rubble in satisfaction, waiting for Sasha to come back from the yard where she had left the sleeping guards and minors. Just as he saw her figure in the low light of the emerging dawn, un-expectantly, another explosion rocked the entire cliffside. The explosion was so strong it sent Sasha flying and even caused Anthony's car to bounce a few feet in the air as he clutched the steering wheel to avoid being thrown through the window. When the rumbling finally stopped, the entire parking lot was riddled with large cracks and the whole mine looked like a giant rock pile. The bridge over the lake that had gone between the mine and shed no longer existed and half the cliff face had fallen into the lake.

Anthony got out of the car to take in all of the damage. As he looked over towards the lake, he noticed a forming whirlpool. All the water in the lake was being sucked into something big that must have opened up with that last blast.

"What did you do!?!" Sasha yelled as she ran up to his car and tried to punch him in the face. He wrestled her back, holding onto her fists.

"I didn't do it! I swear. I set two blasts, not three. I have no idea where that last explosion came from. I swear!" he exclaimed.

"You've destroyed everything!" she yelled.

Anthony had no idea what happened. There was no way that last explosion came from the mine or the shed. It had to have been far deeper, and much further into the mountainside in order to trigger the entire cliff face falling down. The ground began to rumble again, but this time it was coming from a distant hillside. *The shock must have destabilized the entire region! Who knows how much damage would accumulate by the time the destruction hit the full light of day!* he thought.

"I trusted you, and you ...." Sasha began but Anthony quickly interrupted.

"Trusted me? Did you really go and check the floors or did you set that bomb? I know I didn't set the bomb. There was no need, I just wanted to shut down the mine, not destabilize an entire region putting hundreds of people's lives in danger! You are the one playing around with dangerous viruses, not caring about people's lives. You are the one who doesn't care about people's lives." Anthony said, accusingly.

"I saved your life. I helped you with your hair-brained, half-witted plan. I have everything to lose here. My career, my reputation ..." Sasha said as she leaned against Anthony's car, running both of her hands through her hair, clutching her head as if it hurt to even think about what had happened.

The distant rumbling on the hillside stopped and the sun was starting to peak over the horizon. Both Anthony and Sasha were leaning against Anthony's car, trying to take it all in.

"It's over," Anthony finally responded. "We did it, and it is over. So what if our detonations set off something else. It was probably something in the old buried labs that would have probably gone off eventually anyway, and killed everyone working in the mine if we hadn't set if off when we did."

Anthony looked over at Sasha, who looked quite upset still. She was rocking back and forth with her arms crossed over her chest.

"No more viruses. Everything has collapsed and is buried. No one was hurt, I don't think anyone lives on that hillside over there ...I hope," he said as he looked over the landscape and paused for a minute. Had they killed anyone accidently? Whatever the consequence, it would have been more severe had they let things go the way they were with Dr. Steinman in charge and with more mining every day into God knows what was in those labs.

"The murderous, treacherous Dr. Steinman is dead thanks to you and he can no longer kill any more innocent people. You should be happy, Sasha. You can now ask God for forgiveness," Anthony declared as he leaned back against the car next to Sasha, pointing out at the rubble all around, trying to calm her down.

"That is easy for you to say; you can just go back to your life. I have all of those men in the yard as witnesses. When they wake up, I need to be long gone. No one even knows you were here except me and the now-deceased Dr. Steinman," Sasha explained.

"My life will change. The mine is closed. This town will close and everyone will be re-assigned. Everything I have worked for my entire adult life is gone and I will have to start all over. Worst of all, I'll probably even lose my girlfriend. We had just started dating, but I knew she was the one ... but she wouldn't say yes to marrying me when I asked her tonight. She said it was too soon ... So, we will likely get assigned different towns and you know how that goes," Anthony said. Now he was the one running his hand through his hair and looking distraught.

"Well, that's her loss, a handsome man like you could have any girl he wants," Sasha said as she looked up at Anthony with a smile. "Speaking of leaving this town ... I need to get out, quick! At least before those men in the yard wake up and realize what happened. Can I get a ride?" she asked, looking as composed as she could while brushing the dust off of her clothes.

"Sure," he replied as he got in the car. "You know, you did the right thing," he said as she sat next to him in the car. She looked over at him with that sidewise look she favored for a while, then eventually nodded her head in agreement. As they drove out of the parking lot, bouncing back and forth on the cracks all throughout the cement, he looked over to her and said, "Thank you."

She smiled back over to him and said, "Finally!"

~ ~ ~

There was Daniel, in the middle of the hallway, at the high school. He had both hands up and was yelling: "What have you done! Why can't you ever listen!" Right next to him was a man in a wheelchair, looking out at Catherine ominously. He looked like he could be Daniel's brother, but his face and body were so warped with tubes, plates and prosthetics that it was hard to see much of what was human anymore. What was human was covered in black streaks and looked fully integrated into the wheelchair-like contraption in which he was sitting.

Gravity had lost its hold and the whole world felt upside down. *Was this a dream? Really, it had to be!* Catherine thought as she tried to blink away the lights flashing in the hallway full of books and people floating weightless and stunned. Her fellow teacher Elizabeth looked at her in horror and confusion. *As if this was her fault!* Just because the shadowy man at the end of the hallway was speaking to Catherine didn't mean she knew anything about anything.

The only thing Catherine knew was that this wasn't a dream. She couldn't change a thing, she couldn't make anything stop and she had never seen Daniel's brother like this and he had never been in her dreams before. *This had to be real!*

"Why can't this be a dream?" she said aloud. Then it was over. The lights were back to normal. The cyborgs at the end of the hallway were gone, and everything (and everyone) that remained fell to the floor with a thud and a few grunts. Her whole body hurt with the fall and she lay groaning on the floor.

Elisabeth, who was normally peppy and nice, was giving Catherine a mean scowl. She was deadlocked, looking at her for an explanation. The gaze that could kill from Elisabeth was interrupted by Jordan, who clutched Catherine by the arm and dragged her to her feet. In an instant they were heading to the principal's office, as if she was in trouble.

"Jordan, did you see what I saw?" she asked.

A quick nod was all the reply she could get. Elisabeth was up and on her feet, marching right behind them, scowl gone and replaced with bewilderment.

"Do you think he will listen?" Elisabeth asked.

Catherine responded with, "I don't know why; he never listened to me before ..."

Jordon interrupted with, "Yes, but that was before the whole world was turned upside down in front of half the school. How can he not believe you, how can anyone?"

As they reached principal Repalle's office, Jordan let go of his grip and pointed her to go into the room. Catherine entered and opened her mouth to speak but nothing came out.

"You have to stop the mining," Jordan said from behind her. It sounded like a echo of Daniel's warning and jolted Catherine to speak.

"Yes, there is something buried there that needs to stay buried or we are all in trouble. It has to stop now," Catherine explained.

"What do you mean?" Principal Repalle asked.

"I mean, I just saw two cyborgs in the hall yelling about mining waking them up and that we were all going to die!" screamed Elisabeth.

Prinicpal Repalle was on his feet, "Two cyborgs?"

"Yes, and they want us to stop the mining. They have been telling me for months, and I know I told you already and you blew me off but I know your brother runs the mine and you can stop the mining any time," said Catherine.

"You're right. I can stop the mining but that would mean the end of this town and re-assignment for everyone, including my family and we happen to like it here," Repalle responded.

"You won't like it when there are viruses from the mine that kill everyone and everything you know and love ..." Jordan began but was quickly interrupted by the principal.

"Viruses? What do viruses have to do with the mine?" he asked.

"The mining has uncovered buried labs from before the dust where they were experimenting on viruses. The two cyborgs were brothers whose family owned and ran the labs," Catherine explained.

"I see, and they appeared in your dreams to warn you?" Repalle asked.

"Yes, they are in some kind of coma or something I don't know. Daniel would never explain anything. But, they appeared here somehow, in the hallway, today, just now, and threatened to kill us all. We have to stop the mining, we have to shut down the mine," Catherine pleaded.

Repalle looked at the three teachers and after a minute picked up his phone band and opened out the screen for all three to see. He dialed his brother and said only five words: "Shut down the mine, now."

There was silence on the other end, apart from the static of the line, and then finally a response: "Okay. As you wish, brother. It is done. Good day, Sanjay."

"Good day, Alluri," Repalle said as he turned off the screen. "The mine is closed."

"The mine is closed," Jordan said with visible relief as he walked out of the room.

"The mine is closed," Elisabeth said, patting Catherine on the arm as she walked away.

"The mine is closed," Catherine repeated to herself, hearing a faint echo and feeling the room wobble all around her and the lights go dark.

~ ~ ~

Catherine opened her eyes to see a white light above her. She couldn't move her body, and could barely open her eyelids. She tried to speak, but all that came out was a weak, rattling groan. She heard voices to the left and tried to turn her eyes to see.

"They have closed the mine, for good," she heard a soft female voice say.

"I know. What do you think will happen? Do you think you will get Oklahoma? I have family in Wichita. I will probably get assigned there; it is number one on my list," another slightly older female voice replied back.

Catherine felt a gentle hand on her arm as it was lifted to place a blood pressure cuff around her bicep. She felt a small device being placed on her finger, and a thermometer was stuck in her mouth, under her tongue.

"I sure hope I get Oklahoma!" said the first voice.

"I think she is awake, Kate," said the second voice, coming around to Catherine's left side.

"Hi, Catherine, how are you feeling?" the voice that belonged to Kate asked.

"I ... where am I?" Catherine managed to get out as the face of a beautiful young, dark-haired nurse appeared in front of the light.

"Dear, you were in an accident. You were stuck in the rubble of a landslide for two days before the crew was able to pull you out," said the voice to her left. "I'm

Mindy, and this is Kate, and we are the nurses who have been taking care of you. You're in the hospital, dear."

"Mindy! You are scaring her. Look at her heart rate, it just jumped to 145!" Kate exclaimed as she opened up the blood pressure cuff and removed it as well as the device from Catherine's finger and then said, "All of your vitals are looking good. You'll be able to go home in no time."

"What do you remember last, dear?" Mindy asked. She had a sweet face, with pretty, bright blue eyes and fluffy brunette hair.

"I remember ... driving ... an explosion ... did someone ... blow up ... the mine?" Catherine inquired, barely able to get out any of the words, her throat was so hoarse.

"Blow up the mine?" Kate laughed, "What in the world would make you think someone blew up the mine? There was an earthquake that caused a hole to open up under the mine and collapse most of it into the lake. Everyone is saying how lucky it was no one was hurt."

"Except you of course. You see, the earthquake caused the landslide that crushed your car and pinned you ...." Mindy began.

"Mindy! What did I say!" Kate whispered very loudly. "How about I get you a saline drip? You sound a bit hoarse and are probably just a little dehydrated," she continued as she walked over to hang a bag from a nearby hook and then place a connector into the IV in Catherine's left arm. The flush of the IV tasted nasty but the cooling fluid was making her throat feel better already.

"Is ... the mine ... closed?" Catherine asked.

"Yes, it looks like there is so much damage that is just isn't worth it to the company to dig through the rubble," Mindy answered.

"And, they are worried about more earthquakes I think. They just decided this morning. They had been talking about continuing digging all week. The owner of the mine, Alluri Repalle, unexpectedly came on the news and announced it. It was a shock to everyone. We can turn on the news and find out more if you want. Channel 4?" Kate asked as she used a small controller connected to the bed to turn on the far wall to the local news channel.

"Get your assignment sheets ready and updated everyone. We just got word on how they will be handling the re-assignment now that the mine will be permanently closed. They have announced that they will be moving us all out in phases, beginning in two days. My top three are Oklahoma, Grand Rapids, and Lincoln City. How about you, Don?" said a blonde woman with big hair and an even bigger smile sitting at a grand news desk. The man to her left was dark-haired with a few grey streaks and had sad doe-brown eyes. He didn't look nearly as happy as she did, with visibly slumped shoulders.

"Well, Grace. I haven't updated my list in 8 years because when I met my wife I knew I wanted to stay here in this beautiful valley forever. My three kids and I are not looking forward to starting over anytime or anywhere," replied Don.

"Oh, this is so depressing, Kate. I thought you were the one wanting to cheer her up. She's been asleep for a week and this is the first thing we show her?" Mindy interjected as she turned off the TV and went over to the windowsill. "Look, your boyfriend has been bringing you fresh flowers. He should be here soon; he visits every day."

"Boyfriend?" Catherine managed to get out. So, Anthony had made it out of the mine alive!

"Yes, quite the handsome fellow, I say," Kate beamed, and Mindy nodded in agreement.

"You're a lucky lady to have a ..." Mindy started, but Kate interrupted whispering "Not if they don't get assigned the same place."

"Don't worry, he'll be here soon. Just press the nurse button on the controller if you need us for anything," Mindy continued and then she and Kate left the room.

Catherine stared up at the ceiling light, trying to wrap her mind around everything. She couldn't move anything and could barely move her head. She had no idea what damage had been done to her body in the accident, and was afraid to ask. *Had she really been asleep for a week?*

The hallway at school with Daniel and his brother appearing in front of everyone, her and the other two teachers asking the principal to stop the mining ... *It had all been a dream? Truly? Maybe it felt so real and she couldn't control it because she had basically been in a coma? It had felt so real! Was that Daniel's brother, or did she imagine him?* She could never have imagined something so horrible.

"I am so sorry, Babe," she heard Anthony say as he sat down on the chair next to the hospital bed. He leaned over and kissed her softly.

"What ... happened?" she asked.

He was silent for a while, which was not typical for him at all. He must not want to tell her. He got up and closed the door and then came back to sit down.

"I blew up the mine ... I didn't know it would cause a landslide. I didn't know it would ... hurt you," he finally said.

"Why ... why ... Anthony?" Catherine replied.

"They were experimenting with viruses that they had no God-given right to mess with. They threatened my family, and they threatened you. I had to put a stop to the evil. You are the one who told me the mine needed to close," Anthony declared.

"Close ... not blow up ..." Catherine said, weakly. Anthony was obviously very upset.

"How did you even get on that hillside? You were the only one hurt, out of everyone. Of all the people and all the places to be ... I feel like God is punishing me," Anthony replied, mournfully.

"Jordan...house to...help...stop you," Catherine insisted.

"Jordan? That male teacher who wanted you to come over in the middle of the night? Where you at his house?" Anthony asked.

"Yes," Catherine said and then tried to say more but Anthony interrupted before she could get her voice to work right.

"Now it is starting to make sense ... you spent the night at his place, didn't you?" Anthony began, angrily.

"No ... not like that ... I," Catherine tried to get out.

"I see it now. God didn't punish me. He is punishing you for your adultery. I did what was right to protect those I love and those I thought loved me back," Anthony said, righteously.

"Please, no ..."

"Catherine, sin is sin. It was six in the morning when that landslide got to your car. You had to be coming back from his place ... you had to have been at his place all night!" Anthony began, furiously, and then stood up. "I am not God, and I would never punish you like this," he looked down and caught his breath for a moment, then continued, "but what you did was wrong and only God will forgive you." Then he was gone.

Catherine was so angry. Anthony was stubborn to a fault and never did take the time to let her speak, but not even letting her explain? She closed her eyes and groaned. The room now began to shake and the lights began to flicker. She opened her eyes and everything stopped. *Was that an aftershock from the earthquake?*

She took a few deep breaths to calm down. She was probably going to break up with Anthony anyway. They would have likely been re-assigned different cities. And, he had blown up the mine like an idiot! So, it was his fault she was in this hospital bed right now because it was that explosion that caused the landslide. If anyone should be asking for forgiveness, it should be him!

She heard steps coming into her room. The sound of machine gears turning and a mechanical clang as it touched the floor. It sounded like ...

"Miss Newton, we meet at last, in the flesh," said an all-too-familiar voice.

"Daniel?" Catherine asked as she saw his smiling face above hers in the light. Except, his eyes were a warm hazel green. They weren't their usual glowing gold with flashing symbols that crossed his vision. He had a bit of a stubble brown beard too, instead of the neat goatee, and a full head of wavy brown hair instead of the half plate and half shaved head in her dreams. He was wearing a doctor's robe, but underneath his body was still covered from neck to toe in black, including his hands.

"That would be Dr. Jahren, Miss Newton, and you wouldn't be in this mess if you had just listened to me from the beginning," he answered.

"The mine, it's closed," she replied.

"Yes, you did finally close the mine like I asked. Congratulations on that, by the way. I knew you could do it. I couldn't believe they were still going to dig after the collapse. They must have been making pretty good money off of the research they had stolen and didn't want to abandon their treasure trove. Sanjay ended up persuading his younger brother Alluri after your incessant dream haunting over the last week," he elaborated for her. "It seems Sanjay's influence on his brother was the key, as was your ability to influence Sanjay."

"You're ... welcome," Catherine stated. It was all finally sinking in. Her dreams were real. The influence she had in dreams was real, and what she experienced in the dreams was real. It was all real, and it was all also a dream.

"If you had stayed put at Jordan's, I would have come to save you. I wish you would have listened. But, you wouldn't be the exceptional woman I know if you just did what everyone else told you, now would you?" he said, pulling her chart from the wall.

"Now what?" she said, knowing the answer might not be what she wanted to hear but knowing that whatever was going to happen, her entire world would not be the same.

"Like I said before, you are special to me, and now … I have special plans for you," he replied as a spark of gold began to flicker in his eyes.

Thank you for reading.

Please review this book. Reviews help others find Absolutely Amazing eBooks and inspire us to keep providing these marvelous tales.

If you would like to be put on our email list to receive updates on new releases, contests, and promotions, please go to AbsolutelyAmazingEbooks.com and sign up.

ABOUT THE AUTHOR

H.A. Burns lives in a rainy Seattle suburb with her fur babies: a Siberian Husky, an orange tabby cat and an equally scruffy husband. She has been an engineer in the aerospace industry ever since proudly graduating with a degree in Materials Science & Engineering from the University of Washington in Seattle, WA. She has been telling stories to entertain her four siblings her whole life and is constantly coming up with book ideas inspired by dreams, advancements in science and technology, and all the interesting people she meets. Being a busy professional engineer, she would jot down the ideas and say "One Day" to turning them into full novels for many years until a debilitating battle with Ulcerative Colitis stripped her of her ability to do anything else. She realized then that it is amazing what you can do with a laptop on a toilet if you put your mind to it and ignore the smell. Literally making the most of a crappy situation, with literature.

ABSOLUTELY AMA⚡ING eBOOKS

AbsolutelyAmazingEbooks.com
or AA-eBooks.com

97392797R00115

Made in the USA
Columbia, SC
16 June 2018